J Townse
Townsend, Wendy
The sundown rule

$18.95
ocn703173202
05/24/2011

THE SUNDOWN RULE

Wendy Townsend

THE

SUNDOWN

RULE

namelos
South Hampton, New Hampshire

I want to thank Lori Hickerson Carrell for being a great friend,
and for permission to use the marvelous name "Hickerson."
When I was a student at Vermont College, Norma Fox Mazer
read an early draft of this story. Her support and her faith
in my writing about animals and nature meant a lot.

Thank you, Mark. Thank you, Katya and Helen. Thank you, Stephen.

namelos
133 Main Avenue
South Hampton, New Hampshire 03827
www.namelos.com

For my mom, and for the crows

CONTENTS

THE SUNDOWN RULE

The Sundown Rule

Cash, my cat, brought me another dead mouse. I found it with my foot when I got out of bed. After breakfast I put the mouse on top of the food scraps in the bucket and carried it out to the compost heap at the edge of the woods. Since it was spring, the crows were off finding worms and other small creatures that were just waking up. But they weren't far away. From the oak tree behind the shed came a loud *Cah! Cah! Cah!* Another crow answered from across Marl Lake.

Winter mornings a scout crow sat way up in the oak tree and watched our cottage. He'd say, *Cah! Cah! Cah!* every time the front door opened. When he saw me carrying the bucket he'd start up such a wild, raucous cawing it would crack open the cold gray stillness of the winter and make me happy. I knew that crows ate baby turtles and stole the nestlings of other birds sometimes. But that was the way nature worked, and I loved the crows anyway.

Setting aside the mouse and some leftover cornbread so they wouldn't get buried in coffee grounds and oatmeal, I dumped the bucket and called out, *Cah! Cah! Cah!* I got so excited when I called to the crows that my heart beat faster. I almost felt as though I could fly off with them. Again the crow across the lake answered. I heard others cawing, coming closer. They wouldn't come down to the compost heap while I was outside, though.

I walked back to the cottage, rinsed the bucket with the hose, and took it inside, then sat down in a chair by the window to watch. Cash jumped into my lap and started biting at something on his paw. It was probably sticky pitch he got from batting around a pinecone. Soon the scout crow in the oak tree flew to a lower branch. Another landed high up in the maple tree. Though it was spring, there were no leaves on the trees yet, and against the pale sky the crows looked huge and inky black. More crows appeared, as if they'd been nearby the whole time. They bobbed their heads and fluffed their feathers. The scout wiped his bill on the branch the way Dad sharpened a knife on a steel.

I wanted to tell Dad the crows were here. I wished he would come watch with me, but he was at his desk writing, and I knew he needed to be left alone. Dad worked for the Park Service. When he wasn't out in his truck doing his job, he was at his desk writing articles for nature magazines.

The scout crow sidestepped along his branch and lowered his head as if pointing at the dead mouse. Another crow dropped down and walked toward the mouse, stopped, tilted his head, grabbed the mouse in his bill, and flew back up in the tree. Two others came down and took chunks of cornbread. A third swooped down and started pecking through the rest of the scraps. His feathers were especially black and shiny. I wanted to hold him so bad I felt like I would meow the funny way Cash does when he watches a bird at the feeder. But I'd never ever get to hold a wild crow or even touch his black, black feathers. He found an apple core and flew up into a tree with it.

"Lews?" Dad said. "Feel like putting a log on the fire?"

"Sure." I nudged Cash from my lap and went to the woodstove and opened the door. Red coals glowed inside and I felt their heat on my face. Last winter Dad said, "One day we're putting in a gas unit."

"No!" I said. I loved the smell of wood smoke and helping to stack logs and gather branches for kindling. I loved hearing Dad shuffle out in the early morning to stoke the fire, and hearing the clank of the stove door, the soft sound of a log falling on coals.

"Sweetheart," he said, "not *instead* of our woodstove. In addition to it. So that when I get the flu and can't tend the fire, we can turn on the heat."

"I will tend the fire if you get sick."

"But who will do it when you go away to college?"

"I'm not going away to college."

"Oh yes you are."

"I'm not."

Dad laughed. Then he said, "One day you'll want to, I promise. You don't think so now, but you will."

I took a log from the stack and set it on the coals and shut the iron door, careful not to let it clank too loud. Then I tiptoed to my room and held the door open. With his tail straight up in the air, bent at the tip, Cash walked in ahead of me. He jumped up onto my bed and stretched himself out in a patch of sunshine. Sometimes Cash was black as the crows, but sunlight made his coat brown like dark chocolate. I stroked his silky fur and he purred and curled the toes on one paw, then the other, squeezing the air.

My room had a window that looked out on Marl Lake. It was called Marl Lake because the bottom was marl, decayed leaves and wood that had turned into tiny particles of silt that settled instead of being carried downstream. The water was shallow and clear, barely over my head in the deepest parts. But if I stepped in the marl, I'd sink up to my knees, or higher in some places, and the water would get clouded up with all that dark, decayed stuff. It wasn't like quicksand; my feet touched solid ground under the muck. I guessed it would be scary to step in it for the first time, though.

Midday sunshine found its way through the pine boughs and made my room bright and warm and my terrarium all steamy inside, like a miniature tropical forest. I had made it out of an old glass tank we bought at a garage sale, and it sat on an iron stand beside my bed. A red-backed salamander was hiding under a piece of mossy bark in the terrarium.

When I was little I had all kinds of tanks and fish bowls in my room that I set up for the animals I found in the woods and in Marl Lake. I even had a tank full of lake water and plants I brought up in a bucket. I caught snails and dragonfly larvae and crawdads and tadpoles so I could have my own Marl Lake right in my room. I brought in so many animals Dad made a rule called the sundown rule, which said that by sundown I had to let every animal go in the place where I'd found him.

One time I caught a baby snapping turtle scarcely bigger than a quarter. His tail was as long as his whole shell. I put a rock in the terrarium for him to sit on so he could be out of the water. When I brought up some marl for him to hide in, he kicked it up and the water turned murky. But if I waited patiently and held still, the turtle climbed up on his rock, stretched out his neck, and looked all around, blinking his eyes.

Late in the day, when the sun was low in the sky, I reached into the tank and fished out my little snapping turtle and carried him down to the water's edge. He wasn't like baby painted turtles, who flapped their legs in the air so fast I almost couldn't see them. Instead, he reached out with his feet and tried to pry my fingers off his shell.

Dad didn't need to remind me about the rule anymore. Sometimes I kept animals overnight so I could have them near while I slept, but I let them go the next day. I could see that wild animals needed to be outside, where they could find their own food and live in their own homes.

"Time to let our salamander go," I told Cash.

He squinted his green eyes at me and jumped down off the bed and followed me outside. I carried a glass dish with the salamander in it. My hands were too warm and dry and salty for his skin.

Cash went racing down the path into the woods. When I caught up with him he flopped down right in front of me, forcing me to stop and pet him while he rolled in the sand and pine needles. I roughed his fur and slapped him on the butt. He sprang to his feet and raced off again, ears back, tail arched.

The salamander knew right where to go when I set him down near the rotting log that was his home. He headed straight for it, his body going side to side so that the red stripe extending from his nose down to the end of his tail made S-shapes across the brown leaf and pine litter. Cash sat on the path while I watched until the tip of the tail disappeared.

Once I had a baby robin for a few days. The sundown rule didn't apply to him because he wasn't quite ready to be on his own. He still had some soft yellow parts at the edges of his bill, and he sat on my shoulder and ate the worms I dug up from around the compost pile. Then one day I went for a walk with him riding on my shoulder, and all of a sudden I felt him push off and I watched him fly up into a tree. I stood on the path looking at my baby robin perched on a maple branch just out of reach. I could see his breast that was still spotty but turning orange. He flew again, deeper into the woods, and I waved and said goodbye while tears stung my eyes.

Another time I found a green heron. He was flapping and splashing at the edge of the lake. As I got closer I saw that he was stuck somehow, or hurt—otherwise I wouldn't have been able to get so close to a wild bird. When I stepped into the water, he pulled away from me, his yellow eyes wide open, the black feathers on his head raised. His foot was caught. I reached down in the mud and felt around, thinking I might find the steel parts of an old muskrat trap. I touched soft, thick flesh—the neck of a snapping turtle. The turtle let go, and the heron flopped onto the shore. With his feathers all wet and mussed he looked like a skinny green-and-rust-colored chicken with an extra-long neck. He stumbled over his long legs and flapped his wings. The leg the turtle had a hold on didn't look broken, but it was badly hurt. I reached for the bird, and he flapped hard to get away from my hands. I caught him and smoothed his wings to his sides and brought him to me. He squawked and thrust out his neck, aiming for my face. I held him close and pulled up the bottom of my T-shirt to cover his head—that calmed him down. I had to get him back to the cabin and fix his leg, somehow.

I carried the bird pressed against me, one hand under his body, the other keeping the shirt over him. He was so light he felt like a bundle of sticks and feathers. I hurried up the path through the cattails, bumping the ones from last year, making the heads burst and scattering fluffy brown seeds. I didn't see Dad's truck and figured he'd gone into town. That was okay, I thought. I could do this by myself.

Inside the cabin, I pulled a chair out from the table and sat down with the heron in my lap. Slowly I pulled away the T-shirt. The heron's eyes were round, wide open, the black centers big. I tried to tell him not to be afraid, but my voice scared him and my mouth moving did too, and he thrust up at my face again. I covered his head with my hand and then pulled my shirt back over him while I uncovered his injured leg. The wound was open and I could see bone and thin white strands, like on a half-eaten drumstick from a chicken. It made my insides shrink up to see the bone of an animal who was still alive. His leg stayed straight, though, so I was sure it wasn't broken. There wasn't any blood, and I guessed that either he'd bled a lot already or a bird's leg doesn't have much blood. Still, I couldn't just put Band-Aids on. He needed stitches.

I stood up and, holding the bird against my stomach, went into my room to get the sewing basket Aunt Kay had given me. I checked to see if the needles were inside, and I found some thread for sewing buttons on coats. I took the basket to the table and sat down. Keeping the bird in place with my arm, I was able to use both hands to thread the needle.

The wound was like a buttonhole, big as the ones on my winter coat. I tried to think of it that way—that all I had to do was stitch up a buttonhole. With the leg across my hand, I pulled the two sides of skin together, being careful not to catch a tendon. Then I put the needle to the edge of the wound, took a breath, and pushed it into the skin. The heron kept still while I made one stitch and then another, and I began to relax, thinking everything was going to be fine. I moved my fingers up to pinch the skin for the next stitch. But this time when I pushed the needle in, the heron struggled and I had to press my arm down to stop him. Blood oozed out. I knew I was hurting him, and I gritted my teeth. He struggled more and my heart sped up and I was scared and I imagined how it would hurt if someone stuck a needle in me. I wanted to stop, but I couldn't, not now. I wished Dad were here to help. I should have waited for him to come home.

There was blood on the needle and on my fingers, making everything slippery and hard to see, but I had to finish. I kept the bird pressed close while he struggled. I told him I was sorry, even though I knew my voice scared him. Finally, he calmed down. I wiped my fingers and the needle on my shirt and dabbed the wound. Keeping a firm hold on the heron, I pulled the two sides of skin together again and took a breath and pushed the needle into his skin and made another stitch. A little blood came out, but not enough to stop me from making one more stitch, and then the wound was closed—I couldn't see bone. Quick as I could, I tied a knot. I forgot about scissors, so I bent to cut the thread with my teeth. I tasted the heron's blood on the thread, like metal and lake water.

Just as I finished, Dad's truck pulled into the driveway. I couldn't wait to show him the heron, and how I had fixed his leg. I heard Dad's footsteps on the porch. The door opened. "Hi, Lews. What've you got there?"

"A green heron. A snapper had him!"

Dad knelt and put on his glasses and studied the bird's leg.

"Isn't that something," he said. "Lews, you did a good job."

The heron kicked out his good leg and clawed the air. "I don't think I can keep him till sundown," I said. "I think he wants to fly away now."

"Yes, I'm sure he does. Shall we take him back to the lake?"

I nodded yes and stood up.

We went out, letting the screen door slap shut, and we walked down the path to the lake and along the shore, to where the mud and weeds were disturbed.

"It was here, Dad. The turtle had him down in the mud. I stole his dinner."

"You sure did."

"I guess it's time." I pulled away my T-shirt and looked down at the heron. I could see one side of his head. The big yellow eye blinked; the round black center grew and then shrank. In the sunlight, the green feathers on his wings had shiny purple on them. He was a shy, wild bird I might never get to touch again. I didn't want to let him go. He stayed still, his head tucked close to his body. "You can go now," I whispered.

Dad stood perfectly still. He could always do that—hold so still he might be a tree.

I thought maybe the heron couldn't fly after all. I thought, *Maybe I'll get to keep him*, and right then, he pushed against me with both legs and burst out of my arms and flew out over the lake. We watched him go, flying low across the water, his reflection right with him. He disappeared in the cattails on the far side.

My throat closed up. Dad put his arm around my shoulder and hugged me. We turned and walked back up the path to the cottage. I held on to the bottom of my shirt, where it was damp and had some blood on it. I knew it was silly, but I hoped it wouldn't wash out.

BIG NEWS

Dad was at his writing desk all the time, early in the morning before work and late at night after I'd gone to bed. But when spring came and the ice on the lake broke up and melted away, Sunday afternoons were for fishing. We'd pack up cheese sandwiches and lemonade and fishing poles and carry our things to the lake. Cash would follow us down the path and sit near a birch tree to watch us load the canoe and push off. Dad always sat in the back to steer and I sat up front, keeping a lookout for pike and turtles. When we got to a spot somewhere near the middle of the lake, Dad would put the bucket over the side of the canoe so the minnows in it could have cool water. We never dropped anchor, since there were only a few places in Marl Lake where an anchor would catch and hold. Then I'd put a worm on my hook. I hated doing that, and I never used more than one—when my line got cleaned, I was done fishing for the day. Dad would bait the hook on his pole with a minnow and cast the line way out in an arc. The splash of the baited hook always signaled time to be quiet. We didn't talk much on our fishing trips. It was funny, because we talked the whole time we made sandwiches and pulled the canoe down to the water, and we talked again later, when we dragged the canoe back on shore.

One Saturday Dad came home from work early. He put the mail on the table and beside it a bag of groceries. "Let's go fishing."

I unpacked the groceries while Dad changed out of his Park Service uniform. A package of cookies was in the bag. I knew he was excited about something, because we almost never ate store-bought cookies.

It was my favorite kind of day on the lake, with no wind, when the surface of the water stayed like glass. The sun shone overhead and there wasn't any glare; everything was clear. It was like seeing into another world. I folded my arms on the side of the canoe and rested my chin there. Dad cast out his line, and I watched the splash where the hook came down. I didn't feel like fishing, I just wanted to be still and look in the water and be out here, thinking about how the whole summer lay ahead. The canoe drifted ever so slightly, the water slow, finding its way around the lake and finally into the stream that flowed on to other lakes.

Dad wasn't getting any bites and I was happy, because I didn't want the perfect stillness to be broken by the struggle with a fish. We had drifted over by a cluster of water lilies, and under one of the round, flat leaves I saw a baby pike not much longer than my hand. Though he was under the lily pad, the sunlight came in at an angle so his scales were lit up all silvery green, and he cast a shadow on the marl below. He looked kind of like a barracuda, with his long snout and a few pointy teeth showing. The fins at his gills and on his back were slowly fanning in the water. He seemed to be floating in space. I watched the pike's eyes, the black centers round and ringed by silver. I shifted my arm and his eyes began to move, looking around as his position in the water changed with no effort I could see. Suddenly, in a flash of silver-green, he was gone, leaving a puff of marl in the water that looked like smoke.

"Louise," Dad said.

I was surprised by his voice.

"Big news."

"What?"

"I'm going to Brazil to do an article for *National Geographic*."

"That's great! But who will take care of Cash while we're gone?"

"Oh, Lews. I'd love to take you with me, but there's no way.

We're going into the rain forest and it's work the whole time. I can't be worrying about you, about something happening to you."

"Like what, Dad?"

"For one thing, there are deadly poisonous snakes."

"There are massasaugas right here in our back yard."

"Sweetheart, a fer-de-lance is a lot more dangerous than a little swamp rattler. It's just too rugged a trip. Besides, it'll be hot and buggy. You would be very uncomfortable for six weeks."

"Six weeks?"

"Yes, Lews. It's a lot of work."

"Cash and I will be fine, then."

"No," Dad said, "you're going to stay with Aunt Kay and Uncle Jack."

"But what about the compost crows, and the garden?"

"The Lees will tend the garden," Dad said, as if it had been arranged.

"So you already talked to them?" The Lees were our closest neighbors, just down the road.

"Yes, and about looking after Cash, too."

"What?"

"You know your Aunt Kay is terribly allergic to anything with fur. And Cash would not like being away from his life here in the woods."

"Neither would I. I'm not going without my cat!" I yelled, but then my lip quivered and I had to quit right there, because I knew I didn't have any choice.

I didn't talk on the way back to shore, or when we dragged the canoe out of the water. I carried the picnic things inside and let the screen door slap behind me, and I scooped up Cash from the table, where he knew he wasn't supposed to be, but always was when we were out. I heard Dad open the door and come in behind me.

"The Lees will come every day and feed Cash," Dad said. "He'll be fine."

"He won't. I feel sick."

Dad sighed. "Go lie down, then."

I carried Cash upstairs to my room and shut the door. "What are we going to do, Cash?"

He purred and lay down beside me. His eyes shut tight and the purring grew louder as he pushed and pulled on my hair with his paws. I put my arm around him and pulled him closer. He smelled like dry pine needles and moss.

Every Thanksgiving, Dad and I drove down to Aunt Kay and Uncle Jack's for the week. I liked going to visit them, and Dad got to sit on the couch with Uncle Jack and watch football. The only problem was, there wasn't anything for me to do, since they lived on a street where the houses were jammed in close together. But since the last visit they had moved into a big house in a development, and Dad said I might like the new neighborhood. I thought about how nice to me Aunt Kay and Uncle Jack were whenever we visited. Uncle Jack kept the candy jar in the living room filled with my favorite: chocolate-covered peanuts. He would ask me about school and I would tell him, and no matter what, he'd say something good. One time I told him I got a bad grade and he said, "Heck with 'em. They don't know genius when they see it," and we sat together eating chocolate-covered peanuts. Aunt Kay was always fussing and cooking up special treats. She was willing to talk about anything and everything, even stuff like catching tadpoles and salamanders.

One Thanksgiving I had just learned to make pom-poms in art class at school, and I brought my balls of yarn down to Aunt Kay and Uncle Jack's. It was cold and rainy the whole time and I sat on the rug in the living room and made so many pom-poms that I started getting tired of them.

Aunt Kay came into the room with mugs of cocoa for us. "Would you like me to show you how to make a yarn doll?"

"Yes!" I said, and Aunt Kay sat down on the rug beside me and showed me. I made three dolls and used up all my yarn, but Aunt Kay just took me right to the arts and crafts shop downtown and let me pick out all the yarn I wanted, and even some wiggly eyes to stick on the faces. She said, "You need a sewing basket," and she helped me choose one, and needles and thread and buttons to put inside.

Before Dad and I went back home, I gave Aunt Kay one of the dolls. She said thank you and held the doll close, like it was the nicest present she ever got.

But I didn't really want to make dolls anymore. I wanted to be with my cat and my compost crows and my summer on Marl Lake. I didn't know what I would do at Aunt Kay and Uncle Jack's for a whole six weeks.

After a while Dad tapped on my door and I sat up.

"Six weeks isn't so long," he said. "And I'll have pictures and stories enough to last all winter."

I picked at something on Cash's ear.

Dad went on. "Listen, you'll be fine. You might even have fun. Remember, now Aunt Kay and Uncle Jack have a big, new house. You can bet you'll have your own TV in your room, with all kinds of movies and no dad to fight with over what to watch." He chuckled over that.

"We never fight over what to watch," I said back.

"All right, Louise, you know what I'm trying to say. This job is important to me and to us."

I wiped my nose on the back of my hand and looked at my dad. I knew I was being selfish. I nodded my head and said okay.

Goodbye, Cash

The morning we left, I took Cash's collar out of my desk drawer and wrapped it around my left wrist twice. It was red, with a silver buckle. He'd worn it only a week. Dad had said that Cash needed to wear a breakaway collar so he couldn't hurt himself if he got caught on a branch or a fence. But after he lost five breakaway collars in two weeks, we gave up making him wear them. The collar I had around my wrist was the only one I could find. I'd seen one of the crows pecking at something in the cattails, and I went to see. Crows were always messing around with shiny things. Since I didn't have any pockets, I wore the collar as a bracelet.

When the car was packed and we were ready to go, I picked up Cash and carried him inside so he wouldn't try to follow us. I rubbed my face in his fur and breathed in the mossy, earthy smell of his coat. Then I set him down on my chair by the window, where I always sat to watch the crows, and I went out the door and pulled it shut behind me.

Leaving the Park Service truck by the shed, we got into the Volkswagen and Dad started the engine. I turned to look at the cottage one more time. Cash had left the chair by the window and come out his cat door around back, and he sat on the porch, watching us leave. The car followed the curve in the driveway and then Cash and the cottage were out of sight behind the pine trees. I swallowed hard and turned back around in my seat and looked at the road in front of the car. With lunch in a paper sack between us, we headed south toward Indianapolis, where Aunt Kay and Uncle Jack lived.

After a while I asked, "Why didn't they move to the country when Uncle Jack retired?"

"Jack wanted to. But Kay didn't want to give up her volunteer work and activities with the church."

"But they don't go to church."

"No, Kay and I didn't grow up in a churchgoing family. The church plays an important role in the community, though, and she does have a strong belief in community service."

"Is the National Park Service community service?"

"Sort of, but not really. My job's a paying job, and your Aunt Kay does volunteer work."

"What does she do?"

"Specifically? Well, she organizes fundraising events for the homeless, helps with projects to create jobs. I know she raises a lot of money for libraries and recreational centers for kids. Stuff like that."

Since we were there on the holidays, I'd only seen my Aunt Kay cooking and cleaning. I didn't know she did other kinds of work too. But I did know that she and Uncle Jack had a daughter who died. Penny was her name. She was my cousin, and she died right before I was born.

By midday we had passed through pine and white birch forests and swampland, and had entered endless corn and soybean fields. I unwrapped the peanut butter sandwiches we'd packed for lunch. They were thick, on whole-grain bread that Dad and I had baked, and made with organic peanut butter and raw honey. I folded a paper napkin around one and gave it to my dad. Then I opened the thermos of coffee and poured some in the cup and set it down on the armrest between us.

"Thanks," Dad said. He took a bite of the sandwich. "You're going to get spoiled on Aunt Kay's cooking."

"I know." Dad was always making steamed vegetables and

brown rice and fish. Aunt Kay made meat loaf and mashed potatoes with gravy, and she always made dessert—real dessert, not just an apple or an oatmeal cookie.

Dad ate the last bite of his sandwich. "No home-baked bread for either of us for a while."

"That's right," I said. I didn't mind if he felt a little guilty for leaving. "What will the food be like where you're going?"

"No idea. Probably rice and root vegetables. Some meat, maybe fish. Plenty of tropical fruit, I hope. What Brazilians eat and what we get on the trail may be quite different, though."

I sat looking out my window, wondering what would come up in the garden while we were gone. Dad had told the Lees to pick everything they wanted. I was the one who tended our garden, mostly. We grew squash, beans, carrots, lettuce, spinach, and little cherry tomatoes, because our growing season was too short for big ones. The soil was so sandy that every spring we had to take the truck into town, to the farm and garden supply, for bags of manure. Dad helped me get everything started, but he was always too busy working to keep up with the weeding. We made compost all year round. In the summer I dragged up buckets of marl from the lake to add to the compost heap. I tried to add fish heads and guts when Dad cleaned fish for dinner, but the crows always got them. I missed the crows already.

The cornfields had disappeared, and we were on a four-lane highway in the midst of housing developments and shopping malls.

"It's a city, only without tall buildings," I said.

"It's suburban sprawl." With one hand on the steering wheel, Dad unfolded the directions Uncle Jack had given over the phone. "This is our exit coming up," he said, putting on the turn signal. "We go through four lights, make a left, and go one mile. Creekside Court should be on our left."

I sat up straight in my seat, looking out the window to see what my summer here would be like. We drove down a wide, busy street with fast-food restaurants, gas stations, and supermarkets on both sides. I didn't see anyone walking.

"Do they have a bicycle?"

"I don't know, sweetheart."

After Dad made the left turn I started noticing trees and bushes, but in patches, broken up and divided by close-together houses with lawns. Out my window on the right I saw a golf course that went on a long way. There was so much grass, a perfect carpet of brilliant green, and not one weed. Here and there stood a maple or an oak tree, tall and healthy-looking, the branches cut back so that each tree had the same shape as every other.

I had just caught sight of a little pond when Dad said, "Here we are, Creekside Court."

He made a left turn onto a new blacktop road so smooth the tires made no sound. It was as though we'd left the earth and were driving on nothing. All the houses were big and made of bricks with white trim and black shingled roofs.

"Three twenty-seven—this is it," Dad said, stopping the car. He parked and we got out and stretched. The front door of the house opened, and my Aunt Kay and Uncle Jack came out to meet us.

"You poor dears," Aunt Kay said. "You must be exhausted and starving." She hugged my dad and then me, squeezing hard. She felt soft and warm and she smelled like lilac soap. "Oh, my," she said. "We're so happy you're going to be here with us."

I saw that her eyes were moist. "Me too," I said, even though it wasn't really true. But I couldn't be mad at her for Dad leaving.

Uncle Jack said, "Hiya, kiddo," and opened his arms for a hug. His belly had gotten bigger, so I couldn't reach all the way around. He laughed and mussed my hair gently.

"Come in and see the house," Aunt Kay said.

Uncle Jack held the door for us as I followed Dad inside. He put my suitcase and backpack at the bottom of a wide staircase. We both looked up at a huge chandelier with sparkling teardrop-shaped crystals. The ceiling was so high. Just the entryway we stood in was practically bigger than our whole cottage. In the living room there was a stone fireplace that looked as though it hadn't been used. The couch and chairs were thick with velvet cushions, and the lamps had fancy silk shades. Tall windows lined two walls, with drapes that reached the floor. I tried to imagine what drapes would look like on our cottage windows back home. We didn't even have curtains. Then I saw the candy jar—the very same one, and full of chocolate-covered peanuts.

"Quite a house, Kay," Dad said.

"We love it. We've lived here only six months and it feels like it's always been our home." She smiled at me. "And Louise will be the first to stay in the guest room. But let's have lunch before you two collapse from hunger."

Aunt Kay led us into the kitchen, which was so white and gleaming I had to squint. A table was set for lunch with pale yellow cloth napkins and placemats, and in the center was a small vase with one white rose. "The first one from Uncle Jack's garden," Aunt Kay said.

She had made tomato soup and tuna sandwiches on white toast and a salad with green grapes and walnuts in it. It was delicious, all of it. When Dad made tomato soup it wasn't creamy and sweet, it was full of chunks of tomato and herbs and onions. Our salads were always dark leafy greens, never with fruit.

Dad told Aunt Kay and Uncle Jack how much it meant to him that they were having me for the summer.

"Six weeks," I corrected.

Dad shot me a look and my face grew hot.

"I'll be able to focus on my work without having to worry about her," he continued.

"We're just thrilled to have her," Aunt Kay said. Then she brought out a strawberry layer cake with fluffy pink frosting and set it on the table. Uncle Jack leaned back in his chair and patted his round stomach. Dad grinned at me.

"I'll put on coffee," Aunt Kay said.

After lunch I followed Dad upstairs to the room where I would be staying. It was enormous, and so was the bed. I'd never seen one so grand, with four tall bedposts and a pile of pillows and a thick comforter, all in white.

"Wow, Lews, look at this," he said, setting down my things beside a dresser. "A room fit for a princess, complete with your very own bathroom. Look at the size of that TV screen." He put his hands in his pockets and looked around the room. "What do you think?"

"It's really nice."

Dad looked at his watch. "I've got a long drive ahead and packing to do before tomorrow." He hugged me to him and held on tight.

My angry feelings softened. I put my arms around my dad and leaned my head against his chest and smelled the wood stove on his shirt.

"I'll write the first chance I get," he said. He brushed the hair back off my forehead and smiled. "Have a good time, Lews. I'll be home before you know it. And remember to help your Aunt Kay, huh?"

"I will, Dad."

"That's my girl."

I stood on the front steps with Aunt Kay and Uncle Jack and watched my dad drive away.

Aunt Kay and Uncle Jack

"Well," said Uncle Jack. "Guess I'll change into my work clothes and cut the grass."

"Wait!" I said. I didn't want him to leave too. But I was being silly. He was only going to the back yard.

Uncle Jack smiled. "What is it?"

"Do you need help?"

"Pushing that heavy mower is a one-man operation, kiddo." He patted my shoulder. "I bet your Aunt Kay needs help with dinner."

"Oh, you poor dear. You must be so tired from the long trip," Aunt Kay said.

"I feel okay."

"Why don't you unpack and get settled in. Then come down and keep me company and maybe you can set the table."

"All right," I said. It felt like everyone was leaving, going off in different directions, and my stomach had a funny shrunken feeling, even though it was full from lunch. Maybe I really was tired. I climbed the stairs to my room to unpack.

My suitcase and backpack sat beside the dresser where Dad had left them. I opened the suitcase and lifted out stacks of clothes—T-shirts, shorts, jeans—and dropped them in the drawer. Then I scooped up a mound of socks and underwear, dropped that in, and pushed the drawer shut. I hung my one dress in the closet on a pink satin-padded hanger that had a bow on the hook. I tossed my sandals and the extra pair of sneakers onto the closet floor. I doubted I'd ever need Dad's U of M sweatshirt, not in this heat, so

I put it up on the closet shelf along with the suitcase and shut the door. Next I put my hairbrush and toothbrush in the bathroom. On the vanity was a dish of little balls of pink soap shaped like roses. Using them would be like trying to wash up with a handful of slippery marbles.

I heard the lawn mower fire up and I went to look out the window. Uncle Jack was wearing a straw hat with a wide, floppy brim. His white socks were pulled up so high they nearly met his khaki shorts. He pushed the mower, his arms straight out, his stocky legs working and the cut grass zinging out to the side. I could smell the sweet green of it, even through the shut window. We didn't have a lawn back home. Our yard was all sandy dirt and pine needles and patches of skinny weeds.

I took my backpack over by the bedside table and fished around for a book to read later on, before bed. I had brought *Island of the Blue Dolphins* and *Julie of the Wolves* and *Rascal* and *It's Like This, Cat* and a few others. I'd read them all more than once except for the one my dad gave me before we left home. "You'll like it, Lews," he'd said. "There are lots of animals." The book was called *The Golden Compass*. But I didn't feel like reading something new. I picked out *Ajax*, which was my favorite, about a girl who lives on a ranch in the Australian outback. She has all kinds of pets, like birds, tortoises, a kangaroo, a monkey, dogs, and of course a special dog who is part dingo. That's Ajax. I love the part where she's scared she's going to be sent away to boarding school, but then she gets hurt and gets to stay home for another year. Her parents bring in a tutor so she can have school at home.

I sat on the bed fit for a princess and tugged on Cash's collar, pulling it around and around my wrist. Poor Cash, home alone. At least he had the woods and all around Marl Lake to explore. I knew he'd go hunting and bring his prey into the cottage. I could just see his sleek black head pushing through the cat door, with a squeaking rodent in his jaws. Or some poor bird who'd flap and struggle at the windows, desperate to get out. Surely the Lees would help the birds to get out. I hated that I couldn't do anything about it, so far from home. Six weeks. Half the summer. I wondered how I could make the time go by quicker. There were only so many DVDs I could watch, only so many books I could read. I wondered if Dad made it home yet. The clock on the bedside table said four p.m. Two more hours of driving for him. I hoped he was happy, getting to go on such an exciting trip. He said it would be hard work. But I knew he loved it anyway. He'd get to see animals I'd only seen in movies and magazines. I didn't think I could find even a snail around here.

I heard the clank of a pot in the kitchen. I figured I better go downstairs and visit with Aunt Kay. How could I be mad at her when she was so kind to me? It wasn't her fault that she was allergic to cats.

"Aunt Kay?" I called out, entering the gleaming kitchen. But she wasn't there after all.

An oval-shaped slow cooker sat on the counter. I lifted the lid and breathed in the steam rising from a thick stew, bubbling with chunks of meat and carrots and potatoes. It smelled salty and good. I thought I'd try out the ice and water gadget in the refrigerator door, so I opened the cabinet and took out a glass. When I pressed it against one lever there was a mechanical grinding noise and ice clinked into the glass. Then I pushed against the other lever and water flowed down, filling the glass. I took a drink and it was so cold I got a chill. I went to the sink to dump out some of the ice, and I looked out the window at the fresh-cut, brilliant green lawn. Uncle Jack was tending his roses now. He was tying the branches to strings that were nailed to the wooden fence. If all the branches did what Uncle Jack wanted them to, the fence would be covered with green leaves and, when the roses bloomed, white flowers like the one on the table at lunch. It would be wild-looking and different from everything else in their tidy, clean home.

I felt like I was being watched. A spider was up in the corner of the window, peeking out from behind the lace curtain. I knew she was watching me, because she was a jumping spider, and jumping spiders see well.

"Hello, you," I said. She was so black against the pale yellow wall paint, and she had several shiny green eyes. Jumping spiders are not like other spiders that sit still in webs. Those spiders have poor eyesight, and if you touch their webs they scurry down a silk strand into a corner and hide. But jumping spiders watch everything. They turn their bodies to follow what you're doing. When I find a fly and hold him between my fingers, keeping very still, sometimes the spider pounces and grabs the fly, and sometimes she creeps up and gently takes him.

"Should I go try and find you a fly?" I asked the spider.

"All unpacked, dear?" Aunt Kay said, coming out of the laundry room. She wiped her hands on her apron. It was yellow, with white pockets and a ruffle around the bottom.

"Uh-huh."

"Would you like to set the table?"

"Sure."

A fly landed on the counter—a fat one, perfect for the jumping spider.

"Look at that dirty fly," Aunt Kay said, taking the fly swatter from its hook by the sink. It was a yellow plastic one with a white daisy pattern on the swatting part, and Aunt Kay was quick with it. *Whap!* I winced. The fly was a smashed raisin on the mesh of the swatter. Aunt Kay turned on the faucet and washed him down the drain. She tapped the swatter against the side of the sink before putting it back on the hook, and she began humming to herself. I started opening drawers, looking for silverware.

"The second one on the left, dear," Aunt Kay said.

After dinner I was rinsing dishes at the sink when I noticed that the jumping spider had come out again, this time on the window-sill. And before I could say anything, *whap!* Aunt Kay came from behind me and swatted the spider.

"No!" I yelled.

"Oh!" Aunt Kay cried. "What is it?"

I stared down into the garbage disposal, where the spider's body had fallen.

"She wasn't hurting anyone."

"She?"

"The spider!"

"My gosh, I thought it was a fly."

Uncle Jack stuck his head in the door. "Everything okay, girls?"

Aunt Kay shook her head. "Dumb old me, I swatted a spider."

"Now, what in the heck did you do that for?" Uncle Jack said.

"I thought it was a fly! It was black and it moved like one and I can't see well enough without my glasses. I'm sorry, dear. Let me fix you a nice cup of cocoa."

Aunt Kay took out a package of instant cocoa with tiny marsh-mallows, tore off the top, and shook the contents into a mug that had a moose wearing red socks on the side. She filled the mug with milk and put it in the microwave.

I took the cocoa upstairs and sat down on the bed. I wished I could talk to my dad. He says it's bad luck to kill spiders in the house. Back home, we had some really big, hairy-looking spiders—wolf spiders and wood spiders. I loved them, but I didn't want them hiding in my shoes or nesting in my blankets. When they got into my room we'd catch them in a cup and take them outside and let them go by the woodpile that was too rotten to use for firewood.

Once I asked Dad about the bad luck. "What will happen if I kill one by accident?"

"Oh, sweetheart," he said, "nothing will happen. It's just an old superstition. But spiders are beneficial to the environment, and there's no good reason to kill them."

I put on my nightgown and went to the window. There were actually two that opened out, like a pair of French doors. I lifted the levers to unlock the windows and cranked the handles to open them. The screens had little knobs that held them in place. Taking one in each hand I twisted the knobs, and I lifted out one of the screens. Warm, humid air washed over me, still smelling like cut grass. I shut the air conditioner vents, pulled up a chair, and rested my arms on the windowsill. Beyond the roof of the house on the other side of the fence I could see the tops of some trees. Were they in somebody's yard, or outside of the development?

All I could hear was the steady whir of traffic in the distance.

CREEKSIDE COURT

If this was Creekside Court, where was the creek? Surely there would be frogs and crawdads in it. The trick was finding it without trespassing in someone's yard.

There was a narrow cement sidewalk that went all through the development. Something about the sidewalk said, "Stay on me." I followed it up one cul-de-sac and down another, but all I could see was houses and lawns and shrubs clipped so tight they looked like gumdrops. It was like being in the middle of that board game called Candy Land.

Finally I came to what must have been the edge of the development. Looking between the houses I could see what might be a ravine. A little farther on, I came to a house that wasn't boxed in on both sides. To the left, the mowed part of the lawn stopped at a line of gumdrop shrubs. On the other side the grass was uncut and weedy and I figured I could walk there. The ground sloped, the weeds grew thicker, and then I saw what might be a creek if it rained hard enough. A trickle of water ran over stones. I could probably just get the soles of my feet wet. If I turned over a rock, nothing would be under it, except maybe tiny bugs.

I thought of the treetops I'd seen the night before. To get there without going through someone's yard I'd have to leave Creekside Court. I followed the sidewalk to the gate that didn't really close but was there for appearance. Leaving Creekside Court, I went in the opposite direction from the six-lane road and gas stations and McDonald's. The sidewalk continued along the fence surrounding Creekside Court. The fence was wooden and painted gray-green and tall, so that I could see only the second-story windows of the houses. Drapes were pulled shut in the windows.

Across the two-lane road was the golf course, so green in the bright sun that my eyes hurt to look at it. Sprinklers were flick-flicking water all over the grass, making it glisten. Cars went by fast. In the gutter I saw a flattened rag of skin tanned by sun and tires, with patches of fur and bone sticking out. Maybe it was a possum, or a cat. I kept walking up the sidewalk and didn't see any people. They were either in cars that passed by or inside the houses. I had to remember that Creekside Court was a retirement community and I was probably the only kid for miles.

Just then a robin flew in front of me with a bill full of bugs and disappeared into one of the blue spruce trees that had been planted in a row along the fence. When I got closer to the tree, he flew back out and scolded me with a loud *chirp*-chirp-chirp-chirp. Carefully I pulled a prickly branch aside and saw the mud-and-grass nest, but it was too high up to see inside. I could hear the babies peeping. If only I could hold one of them, just for a moment. But I didn't want to risk breaking the mud rim by trying to reach it. The robin scolded, *chirp*-chirp-chirp-chirp!

"Okay, okay," I said. I walked away from the nest and kept going. Then the sidewalk stopped and Creekside Court ended. The fence turned a corner where the last house was, and the trees I'd seen out my bedroom window grew along it in a narrow patch of woods. Wild blackberry bushes made a stickery hedge between the trees and a wide-open sort of field that had been cleared and scraped down so that it was flat. Patchy weeds were starting to grow back around scraps of plywood and roofing material and flattened-out cardboard boxes that were strewn around. There were more houses beyond the field on two sides.

I stepped off the sidewalk and entered the patch of woods. I felt like I was in a capsule, hidden between the trees and the blackberry hedge. A crumpled white McDonald's bag stuck to the ground, stiffened and matted down by rain. Ahead I saw the tallest of the trees, an enormous tree with branches reaching out and up into the sky. I didn't know what kind it was. When I tried to put my arms around the trunk I saw that there needed to be one more of me, with arms outstretched, for our fingers to touch. I leaned my cheek against the smooth bark that was all different shades of gray. The tree felt solid and strong as iron. Maybe they had tried to cut it down, but it broke their chainsaws. There was a hole in the tree, around to the side. On my tiptoes I could just reach the rim. I stood back to see if I could look in the hole, but it was too high up. Back home, there was never an empty hole in a tree—some creature always made it into a home. But maybe here, there weren't any animals left who could climb up the tree and use the hole.

A Styrofoam cup was wedged between the tree's roots. I frowned and kicked it out of there. Looking around, I saw more trash and figured it must have been blown in by the wind, since I didn't see any footprints except my own.

I walked back to Aunt Kay and Uncle Jack's house. The sun was overhead, and I started feeling hot and thirsty. I kept up with my shadow on the sidewalk as I went through the gate and past the houses. I was thinking about what kind of animal could be living in that hole in the big tree. A frantic thrashing of leaves startled me and a rabbit darted across my path, over the blacktop and into someone's front yard, where he froze, sitting up like a chocolate Easter bunny. Something caught my eye a little way from where the rabbit had been—a pale bit of fur sticking up. I wanted to go look, but it was close to somebody's house, at the edge of the flowerbed. All the drapes were pulled shut, and so was the garage door. I stepped onto the grass. I kept one eye on the bit of fur and the other on the front door of the house. As I came closer I saw that there was more fur on the ground, sort of mixed in with dry grass. I knelt and lifted the patch of furry grass and caught my breath.

Baby rabbits were crammed into a bowl-shaped nest right in the ground. I counted five babies, with ears that lay flat across their backs. The whole mass of fur and ears moved with their breathing. I put my hand over the babies, not quite touching, and I felt heat coming from them. I touched the little ears on one of them. I wanted so much to hold him. I turned around to look for the mother rabbit, but she was gone. Surely she would come back to take care of her babies. I wished I could tell them that she would, that everything would be okay.

I slipped my fingers down into the wriggling warmth of their furry bodies. I curled a finger under one of the babies and lifted him out. He kicked out his back feet. His fur was mostly brown, but on his belly it was the color of coffee with milk and his tail was a tuft of white. His paws and feet were the size of my pinkie finger, and his eyes were dark and wet. He tried to shut them and he kicked out his back legs again. I cupped my hands under him and held him against my stomach and he wriggled and curled into a ball. I wished I could take the baby rabbit to my room, just for a little while, just to hold him and look at him. I opened my hands. He trembled and tried to make himself smaller. Keeping my hands cupped around him, I lifted him to my face and breathed in. He smelled like dry grass and fur, not like Cash's fur, but still, earthy and sweet. I wanted to take him to my room for a little while, not even until sundown, because I knew he needed his mother. Again I looked around and could not see the mother rabbit. No one was watching. I covered the nest back up with the quilt the babies' mother had made from grass and fur, and I stood up and carried the baby rabbit back to the house.

I was halfway up the stairs when Aunt Kay said, "What have you found, Louise?"

"A baby rabbit. There's a nest in the neighbor's yard. I was just going to hold him for a minute."

"Oh, my. I really can't have animals in the house. I'm so allergic!" She sneezed right then and pulled out a Kleenex from her apron pocket. Then she smiled and said, "Please take it back outside, dear."

"All right," I said.

With the Kleenex over her nose and mouth, Aunt Kay held open the door for me. I carried the baby rabbit out of the house and down the sidewalk. I didn't see how Aunt Kay could be so allergic. How could rabbit hair have reached her nose so fast?

Back at the house where the nest was, I knelt and lifted the grass-and-fur quilt. I rubbed my cheek against the baby rabbit and then tucked him back in the nest. I stood up and walked away feeling sad. But that was silly. It was best for the rabbit to be with his brothers and sisters and not up in a strange room with a giant girl cuddling him. What was the point of having him in my room even for a minute? I knew I couldn't keep him, even if Aunt Kay let me. He needed his real mother. I heard a crow say, *Cah! Cah!* and I stopped and looked at the sky and saw the black bird way up high, flying fast. Soon he was out of sight.

But I Can't Pet Goldfish

Dad was right—I was going to get spoiled on Aunt Kay's cooking. And Uncle Jack must have said a dozen times, "If you need anything, you just ask your old Uncle Jack." Then he'd pat my shoulder and go out to the garage, or to tend his roses.

It seemed like Aunt Kay and Uncle Jack were busy all the time. Stuck to the refrigerator door with four magnets shaped like pineapples was a calendar with Aunt Kay's schedule on it. Just about every weekday was filled in with events, or places she needed to be and the times she needed to be there.

"The phone numbers are there," she said, "so you can reach me if you need me."

Beside the calendar was another number. "Here is your Uncle Jack's office number, just in case. I can't tell you his schedule, though." She rolled her eyes. "Ever since he retired he wanders in and out of that office any old time he feels the inclination."

Aunt Kay cleaned and did laundry, but she didn't want me to help much. I folded laundry and set the table when we ate, but sooner or later she'd say, "You don't want to be doing this, not on your summer vacation."

I tried to help Uncle Jack with his roses, but the bushes were small and the young shoots were fragile. I could tell that I made him nervous when I handled them. I watched my uncle take the pale green shoots lovingly between his thick fingers and attach them to the strings that were nailed to the fence. He was so happy tending his roses. When I put down the spool of twist ties I'd been holding and went back in the house, he didn't notice.

I went to the place where the big tree was, taking along a plastic bag, and picked up trash. Then I found a flat rock and rolled it to the tree. I sat down with my back against the trunk and fiddled with Cash's collar, pulling it around and around my wrist. I wondered what he was doing. Probably digging little piles in my garden, tearing up the new seedlings. Cash loved to climb the fencepost and jump down into the garden and come rushing to me, tail straight up, and then throw himself down and roll on the sprouted lettuces, purring wildly. Dad always teased me. "Cash helping in the garden today?"

I figured my dad must be in Brazil by now, getting into his big, important work. I knew that I should have a better attitude about it, but it was so unfair that he wouldn't take me with him, like I couldn't take care of myself. I bet he was having such a good time, he forgot all about me.

Aunt Kay showed me her sewing room, which was down the hall from my room and about the same size. It didn't have a huge princess bed, just a small one next to the window, with frilly pillows heaped on it. I noticed the yarn doll I'd made a couple of years before propped against one of the pillows. The doll wore a dress made of green satin.

"Here's my good old machine," said Aunt Kay. It was a plain-looking beige Singer, and it sat on a long table against the wall. "I should buy a new one with all the bells and whistles, but I just can't seem to let go of this one."

All kinds of sewing things were arranged on the table. There was a box of patterns in envelopes lined up like recipe cards in a catalogue. Bolts of fabric lay stacked to one side. There were clear plastic boxes of pins, buttons, a pin cushion you could wear like a bracelet, squares of cardboard wrapped with lace, and different kinds of scissors.

"Do you make a lot of clothes?" I asked.

"Not anymore. I make crafts for the church to sell, mostly. It's no fun making clothes for this old body." She took a piece of lace trim in her hand. "I loved making dresses for my Penny."

I looked at the ceramic horse statues on the shelf across the room. Pinned up on the wall were the blue and pink and red ribbons Penny had won in horse shows.

Aunt Kay went to the bed and sat down. She picked up the yarn doll. "I couldn't resist making her a dress out of some scraps of satin."

I sat down next to my aunt. "It's pretty."

"Would you like to make more dolls? I'll take you to the arts and crafts shop."

"Not really."

"How about sewing a dress? We could pick out a pattern and fabric."

"Maybe," I said. I thought she'd be disappointed if I said no again.

She could tell. "That's okay, dear." She patted my hand and set the yarn doll back in place against the pillow.

"Thanks, though," I said.

One rainy morning I went back into Aunt Kay's sewing room. I stood looking at the shelf with the horse statues. The gray light made them kind of scary, like they might come to life. There were three of them, glazed shiny black. Two had white socks and the third a white patch on his forehead, and they were big, half the size of Cash. One stood as if waiting. One was in mid-gallop. The one with the white patch was bucking, hind quarters in the air, head down, mane and tail wild. I reached up and touched the tail. It felt cool and like glass. I tried to imagine what it was like for Penny to go up in the air and come down wrong. Did she know in that instant that she was going to die? Dad said it was quick, when you broke your neck like that. I didn't know how Aunt Kay could stand to see those horse statues. Didn't she ever want to smash them? And the books on the shelf next to the statues were all horse stories, like *Black Beauty, White Ghost Summer,* and *Justin Morgan Had a Horse.* Why weren't they and the show ribbons put away in boxes? It was strange seeing Penny's stuff as if she was around somewhere, maybe at summer camp or just outside playing. She hadn't even lived in this house. I opened the closet. It looked normal, not stuffed with kid things. For some reason I felt relieved. A stack of neatly folded sweaters in plastic bags sat on a shelf. Clothes hung on the rod, but they were grown-up things, and no small shoes were on the closet floor. Up on the top shelf I saw an empty aquarium.

Later, Aunt Kay pulled peanut butter cookies out of the oven. The house was so air-conditioned that she could bake all she wanted, and she did. It was nice, the way the house smelled like butter and sugar baking. I sat at the kitchen table with her, eating the warm cookies. She had a cup of tea and I had milk. I asked her about the horse statues.

"It wasn't the horse's fault Penny died," she said.

"Were you allergic to horses, too?"

"Oh, yes." She smiled. "One time I picked up Penny's sweatshirt off the floor and shook it out and I had the fit of my life, sneezing and coughing. My throat closed up and I had to get to the hospital for a steroid shot. After that Penny had to do her own laundry."

"Wow," I said. I felt bad for having mean thoughts about her allergies when they really were serious. "There's an empty aquarium in the closet."

"Penny adored her goldfish. She had names for them and she talked to them. I used to hear her..." Aunt Kay sat up in her chair. "You could have that aquarium. I'll take you to the pet shop and you'll pick out some pretty fish. Penny loved those fat white ones with orange mottling that waddled when they swam. You can have any kind you like and we can set that aquarium up in your room."

"But I can't pet goldfish."

One day an odd package came. It was a white cardboard tube that stuck out the end of the mailbox. I recognized my dad's handwriting, always slanty and hard to read. There was no return address, just a postmark from Brazil and three stamps with bugs on them. One showed a blue butterfly, one a black-and-yellow-striped spider, and another a shiny green beetle with long antennae. After peeling away the tape from one end, I pulled off a plastic cap and looked in the tube. A smell of someplace else came out, sort of like hay. I tipped the tube, and a little packet wrapped in paper towels slid down toward the opening. Then I shook the tube, and out came the little bundle and a curled piece of paper that I knew was a letter.

I could tell that something else was inside when I reached in and felt glossy paper. I pulled it out. It was a poster of rain forest animals. And there were leaves and flowers and insects, all with tiny details and bright colors, like orange, red, yellow, blue, pink, and more shades of green than I could count. There wasn't one bit of space that wasn't filled with something alive. Underneath the rain forest scene was a line drawing of it, with all the bugs and animals numbered, and beside that a list of their names. I read Dad's letter.

Dear Lews,

I found these things in the gift shop at the place where I stayed my first couple of nights. I thought you might like the turtle. Actually, I think he's supposed to be a tortoise. How about that jaguar in the poster, huh? He's what we're all hoping to see.

The group I'm traveling with has arrived, and by the

*time you get this we should be well on our way into the
forest. I'm so excited, Lews, and so proud of you for helping
by agreeing to stay with your aunt and uncle. I know how
much you miss your kitty. And I know the Lees are taking
good care of him.*

*I don't know when I'll get another chance to write, but
if I can I will. Say hello to Kay and Jack for me. I miss you
so much already.*

Love,
Dad

I looked at the jaguar in the poster and wondered what it would
be like to walk in the forest and see a cat so big and alive, all spotted,
black and orange. I wouldn't be scared at all. I'd keep very still and
watch him and maybe he wouldn't run away. I tried to imagine
what his fur would feel like.

I opened the taped-up bundle that had been inside the tube and
lifted out a turtle, made of shiny white stuff like ivory. I read the
little card attached by a string, and it said the tortoise was carved
out of the seed of the ivory nut palm, called jarina. The tortoise was
on a black cord necklace and I put it on.

THE RACCOON TREE

Every night after the house quieted I got out of bed and sat by the window. One night I heard a sound like crying. I thought it came from the patch of woods. I tucked back my hair and leaned toward the sound, holding my breath, straining to hear. I heard my heart thumping and then the cry again, faint and wavering. It wasn't human, and it was definitely coming from those trees. But it was too late at night to go out there. I didn't want to make any trouble for Aunt Kay and Uncle Jack. I held perfectly still to try to make out the sound more clearly, but it had stopped. All I could hear was the distant whir of cars on the highway.

Roaring engine noise woke me early the next morning. I looked out the window and saw Uncle Jack pushing the lawn mower around the yard. I remembered the crying sound and pulled on shorts and a T-shirt and sneakers and hurried downstairs.

"Yoo-hoo! That you, Louise?" Aunt Kay called out. She was in the kitchen, and I wondered how she'd heard me when I'd come down the stairs so quietly. The kitchen smelled like coffee and toast and some sort of cleanser. The dishwasher churned.

Aunt Kay pulled the sliding glass door shut on the lawn mower noise. She held a wad of paper towels in one hand and a spray bottle of blue window cleaner in the other. "Oh, there's so much glass in this house," she said. "I hope your Uncle Jack didn't wake you. The ladies from bridge club are coming for lunch and he had to get the mowing done early."

"It's okay."

"Can I fix you breakfast?"

"No, thanks, there's something I need to go see right away."

"Well, all right. Don't go too far, now."

"I won't. I'm just going up the road a little way."

I went out the front door, and it occurred to me that I ought to bring gloves, in case it was an animal that would bite. In the garage I found a box with gardening gloves, and I stuffed one for my right hand in my back pocket. Then I hurried out of Creekside Court and ran all the way up the sidewalk to the trees.

Stepping off the sidewalk's end I started down the path slowly, looking into the brambles in case an animal was hiding there. I stopped every few feet to listen and look up into the trees, wondering if there might be an owl's nest with a hurt baby owl in it. Just ahead was the big tree with the hole in the trunk. I put my hand on the smooth, pale bark. "Is anybody home?"

Then I heard it—the crying, now more like whimpering, and it *was* coming from inside the hole.

"I found you!" I called out, stepping on the rock I'd rolled over. I still couldn't reach whatever was in there, crying and needing help. There were at least two animals crying, two voices. On my tiptoes I could just get my hand into the opening.

I looked around, trying to figure out what to do. I couldn't run back to the house for a stepladder because I would have to explain what it was for. In the field on the other side of the briars I saw more big rocks, turned up by the bulldozer. If I stacked some, I could stand on them and reach the hole. The briars were thick, and I was wearing shorts, but going around to the field on the path and lugging rocks back that way would take forever. When the whimpering grew weaker, I crouched and went through the briars, pushing down the thorny branches and stepping on them as I went.

It didn't take long to find a few rocks that should work. They were too heavy to lift, so I rolled them end over end. By the time I'd moved the rocks through the briars to the base of the tree, I was sweaty and all scratched up. I stood for a moment, pulling briars and leaves out of my hair. All I had to do was stack the rocks. My palms got scraped, but finally I had my rock steps in place, and when I climbed up on top, I could see inside the hole.

For a second I hesitated, a little scared about putting my face in a hole in a tree. What if I saw something awful in there? What if the animals were hurt and I couldn't reach them? How would they feel when they saw a giant face looking down on them? But I had to help if I could. My head blocked some of the light, but there was enough to see the two small faces close together with shining eyes and black masks looking up at me. No bigger than tiny kittens, they held still, huddled against the inside of the hollow that was their nest. I had to get them out of there and hold on to them and feed them.

I pulled the glove from my back pocket, put it on, and reached into the nest. I touched fur and heard a cry as one of them slipped away. With my arm inside the tree, I couldn't see what was happening. I pulled it back out and caught a glimpse of a ringed tail disappearing up another hole in the tree I hadn't seen. It went up inside a hollow branch. When the other baby tried to follow, I grabbed him by the legs. He squealed and let loose of his bowels. I smelled the sharp stink of his fear. He tried to bite through the glove, but his teeth were too small to break through. He fought and struggled, but I had him and pulled him out of the hole, into the light. Taking the baby in my other hand, I turned him around to see his face. We looked at each other. He had dark, bright eyes that *knew*. In that moment he knew that I wasn't going to hurt him and he quit being afraid of me and he quit struggling and went limp and began to cry for his mother.

I shook the glove off my hand and held the baby against my chest while he fretted and cried, and I cried, too, because I knew for sure that his mother was dead. I looked back in at the hollow branch where his brother or sister had disappeared. I couldn't hear anything and I knew he wouldn't come back down as long as I was there. The baby in my hands felt light and feverish. His fur was wispy and dry. I stepped down off the rock, wiped my face with the back of my wrist, and carried the raccoon back to the house.

I could go in through the garage and into the kitchen, but if Aunt Kay was there, she'd catch me and make me take the raccoon outside, like the baby rabbit. I went in the front door, heading for the stairs, but as soon as I stepped into the entryway it hit me. There were cars parked outside. I heard voices.

"Oh, my!" someone cried. A white-haired lady in a blue pantsuit stood there with her hand pressed against her chest.

"That you, Louise?" Aunt Kay called from the dining room. "Come say hello, dear."

My heart thumped and my face felt hot. I walked into the dining room filled with dressed-up ladies at tables. I could feel the scratches on my arms and legs and I could smell the raccoon. Everyone was staring.

Aunt Kay cleared her throat. "My niece is an animal lover."

Some of the ladies laughed.

"Louise, dear," Aunt Kay said, "please take your little friend outside. I'll be right there."

I turned and walked back out the front door. I didn't know what to do, except that I had to get milk for the baby.

"Louise?" Aunt Kay stuck her head out and frowned at the baby raccoon in my arms. "Put it in the garage and we'll figure out what to do later. Come get washed up and have some lunch. I've set a place for you."

I took the raccoon to the garage and found a box and some old towels and made him a nest. He whimpered when I tried to put him in the box, and I got mad at my Aunt Kay.

"I have to go," I explained to him. "But I'll come right back, I promise." I pried his little paws off me and gently pushed him down inside the box. He stood on his wobbly legs and whimpered louder, and all I could do was close the box.

I ran up the stairs two at a time, kicked off my sneakers and pulled off my dirty clothes and threw them in a heap on the floor. Then I went in the bathroom and ran hot water and scrubbed my arms and legs and face with a washcloth. I put on clean shorts and a T-shirt and went downstairs barefoot.

Aunt Kay poured me a glass of milk and gave me a plate of chicken salad with raisins and walnuts on a bed of lettuce. The table was set with a white cloth. I took my napkin out of the silver ring and put it in my lap.

The ladies asked questions about my father's trip to Brazil. I ate as fast as I could, remembering to swallow before I spoke, while I tried to figure out how to feed the baby raccoon.

As soon as my plate was empty, I gulped down half my milk. "Aunt Kay? May I please be excused?"

"Yes, dear," she said.

I took my plate and glass of milk to the kitchen. I got a jar from the cabinet and mixed warm water and milk in it, and I found Q-tips in the laundry-room closet where Aunt Kay kept paper towels and other supplies. I got a hand towel from under the sink and held it under hot water and wrung it out, and then I went out the kitchen door to the garage.

The baby cried and whimpered while I knelt on the floor and opened the box and lifted him out. He calmed when I held him close. "I'm sorry I took so long," I told him. I wiped his belly and tail and feet clean with the damp towel. He wriggled, but he didn't fight too much. Cradling him against me with one arm, I dipped the cotton swab in the milk and held it near his mouth. A drop fell on his lips and he licked them and then he reached for the swab with his tiny paws and sucked on the cotton tip.

Again and again I dipped the cotton tip in the milk and the

baby raccoon drank. After a while he yawned and I saw his pointy white teeth just poking through and his tongue that was thin and pink as a rose petal. His eyes were sleepy-looking and glassy. I tried to put him in the box so I could go back to the tree and see if the other baby had come down out of the branch. Again he clung to my hand, and when I pulled him off he cried and tried to climb out of the box. I picked him back up and held him close.

Clearly I'd just have to stay out in the garage. It smelled a little like gasoline and cut grass from Uncle Jack's mower, and the fluorescent tubes hanging from the ceiling made cold light, but I didn't care. Holding the baby in one arm, I opened the door to the back yard and dragged in one of the patio chairs. I set it by the open door and sat down. The baby fussed and wriggled, making little purring sounds, and finally he calmed and fell into a place somewhere close to sleep. His fuzzy belly heaved up and down with each breath.

Aunt Kay found me after the luncheon was over. "Is it asleep?" she asked.

I nodded my head.

She came closer and put her hands on her knees and bent to see him. "My, he's just a baby," she said softly. "He needs his mother."

"I know," I whispered.

Aunt Kay smiled at the baby and then she straightened herself. "I better call the Humane Society. They will know what to do."

"No, you can't!" I said, waking the raccoon. He whimpered and blinked his shiny eyes. "Can't I keep him? I can bring in one of the benches and sleep on that. Please?"

"Louise, I cannot let you sleep in the garage. Dear, I know you care, but this is not your responsibility. We must let professionals deal with it." She went inside the house.

My baby raccoon fussed and I gave him more milk.

Aunt Kay came back after a little while. "Louise," she said, "a nice lady from the Wildlife Rehabilitation Council is coming to take the raccoon."

I held the baby close and gritted my teeth to keep back tears. I couldn't argue with my Aunt Kay. Maybe she was right, but it still wasn't fair.

When the lady came for the raccoon she put him in a cage that sat on the passenger seat of the truck. At least there was a soft towel inside. She said her name was Margie, and she asked me questions about exactly when and where I found him.

"I doubt the other one will make it," she said. "This one is dehydrated and wouldn't have made it through another night." Margie reached in and petted him. "We're not supposed to touch them unless it's absolutely necessary, but it's hard to resist." She shut the cage door. "The more we touch them, the harder it is to rehabituate them to the wild."

I put my finger through the cage wire and touched his paw. Aunt Kay put her arm around me.

"Don't worry," Margie said. "He'll be fine." Then she got in the truck and drove away.

"Come," said Aunt Kay. "Let's have a nice piece of lemon cake."

The dishwasher was running and the dishes that wouldn't fit were rinsed and stacked for the next load. Tupperware containers sat on the counter, filled with leftover salad. My aunt sat me down at the kitchen table and cut a slice of cake and poured a glass of milk. She fixed herself an iced tea and sat down with me. "How fortunate that you found him, dear. He would have died."

I picked up my fork and broke off a bite of cake and pushed it around on the plate.

"My brother—your father—brought home all kinds of animals when he was a boy," she continued. "And because of my allergies he could not bring them into the house. He wanted a pet so bad you could just about reach out and touch his wanting. Like with you."

"But what did he do?"

"Well, he had to keep them in the garage."

"So why couldn't I? Cash could've stayed in the garage, and I could've kept the raccoon."

"The raccoon is a wild animal. As for Cash, do you think it would have been fair to ask him to leave his home in the woods, with all that freedom, and come live in a garage?"

"It was only for six weeks."

"But dear, this is different. When Jeff and I were growing up, our family lived in a house in an old neighborhood. The street was lined on both sides with grand old maple trees. Ours was the last house on a dead-end street, and cars didn't go speeding by. We had a ravine out back with a thicket of briars and weeds. The garage had a window with a broken pane where a cat could come and go."

I took a bite of cake. It was just the right mix of sugar and lemon and cream. "You said there were other animals?"

"Your father and strays had a way of finding each other. Of course, some of them were sick and we couldn't afford vet bills. Finally Jeff was allowed to keep one pet, but the others had to go to the animal shelter. You can imagine how hard it was for him to choose. Jeff had wanted a dog, but he reasoned that a dog would be unhappy if he couldn't come inside, while a cat wouldn't mind so much. And so your father had his cat. Still, no animal could come in the house. I felt bad, and not just for Jeff, but for me too."

"Why?"

"I had to give up my very first pet before I even had the chance to know her."

"Really?"

"Yes, a little gray kitten. I laid eyes on that kitten and that was it. I picked her up in my arms and didn't want to let go. I think she felt the same way about me, because she purred and purred and nuzzled my chin."

"Cash does that too," I said, pushing my fork around to get the last bits of lemon frosting off the plate.

"Well, after five minutes I started sneezing and coughing and my face swelled up and I couldn't stop. That was my first experience going to the emergency room for my allergies. The doctor told Mom and Dad that I could not possibly have animals in the house. I nearly died of grief when my dad took that little kitten away from me."

"That's awful."

"It was such a long time ago and I can still remember that soft fur." She took a drink of tea. "Enough about that. Did you like the cake?"

"It was really good."

"Now, during lunch, Mrs. Melvin was reminding me that Mrs. Hickerson has a daughter about your age. They go to Grace Missionary Church, out on Route 42. Perhaps the two of you should meet."

"Okay," I said.

That night I sat in the chair at the window in my room, listening for the other baby raccoon. I listened hard, trying to hear him the way I did the first night, even trying to slow my heartbeat and hold my breath. In the dusky sky I could just see the tall branches of the raccoon tree, dark and leafy.

In the morning I went back. I stepped up on the rocks and looked inside. The nest was empty. I stepped down and looked up at the branch the other baby had climbed into. It was nearly as big as a whole tree. If I got a ladder tall enough, I wouldn't know what part of the branch he was in, and even if I could chop it off the baby would be killed when it came crashing down. I banged against the trunk with my fist, hoping to wake him. The tree was so solid it was like pounding on rock. Anyway, if he were still alive, his cries would be too weak to hear.

I don't know why, but I went back to the tree every day and stepped up on the rocks and looked inside the hole. I kept thinking I would look down inside the nest and see a skeleton curled up, with a skull attached to a line of white vertebrae with bits of fur sticking here and there. Maybe he came down and an owl got him. That would be better than slowly starving way up inside that branch— or maybe for him it was like drifting away. Maybe he'd climbed all the way up inside that branch and looked out at the stars through a crack while he drifted off to sleep and never woke up.

SARAH

I was in the kitchen helping Aunt Kay put away the breakfast things when the doorbell rang. "I bet that's Sarah and her mother," Aunt Kay said. "Dear, why don't you go see?"

I opened the front door and saw a woman and a girl in Sunday clothes standing there.

"Hello," said the woman. "You must be Louise. I'm Mrs. Hickerson, and this is my daughter, Sarah."

Mrs. Hickerson had a see-through scarf over her puffy brown hair, but Sarah had red hair. She was wearing a pink dress and she had freckles everywhere, pale blue eyes, and a great big smile. "Hi!" she said. "I like your turtle."

"Thanks," I said, touching my necklace. "It's supposed to be a tortoise, but it looks like a turtle to me too. From Brazil."

Aunt Kay came up beside me. "Hello, Joy. Please come have coffee."

"I'd love some, thank you. But just a quick cup. We can't stay long."

"I have a poster from Brazil too," I said. "It's got all kinds of rain forest animals. You want to see it?"

"Yeah!"

"Sarah," her mother said, "just a few minutes, okay?"

"Right, Mom."

We ran up the stairs and down the hall to my room.

"Wow," Sarah said. "You've got a nice room."

"Yeah, it's pretty big. I like my room back home better."

"Where's that?"

"Marl Lake, up in Michigan in the middle of the woods. It's real wilderness there, with great big pine trees. My cat's there too. His name's Cash and he's black all over, with green eyes. This is his collar." I held up my wrist to show Sarah.

"Why didn't you bring him?"

"My Aunt Kay's allergic. She has fits and has to get a shot if one single animal hair gets in the house."

"I'm allergic too, but not that bad. My eyes get watery and sometimes I break out. I just take an antihistamine."

"I'd die if I couldn't have animals."

"You should be a veterinarian when you grow up."

"I thought about it. Or a wildlife biologist. Then I could go study animals in the rain forest. Anyway, here's my poster. Aunt Kay put it in the frame. She likes things to be neat."

Sarah studied the animals. "They must have a lot of ants in the rain forest to have three kinds of anteater."

"Yeah, I think so. There are a lot of bugs, for sure."

"The jaguar is beautiful."

"My dad's with biologists, tracking them."

"The only place I ever saw a jaguar was in the zoo."

"I've never even seen one, except on TV. But I will, one day. My dad promised to take me next time. Hey, you know what? I had a baby raccoon."

"You did? Where?"

"I heard him crying, out in that big tree." I pointed out the window at the treetop. "His mom died."

"That's terrible. How did you find the baby?"

"There were two down inside a big hole in the tree. But one got away up into a branch where I couldn't reach. I caught the other and brought him back, but I couldn't keep him on account of Aunt Kay's allergies."

"So what happened?"

"A wildlife rehabilitator took him. They'll raise him until he's old enough to go free."

"Sarah!" Mrs. Hickerson called from the bottom of the stairs. "Time to go."

"Hey," Sarah said to me. "Come to church."

"Okay, but I'm not dressed for church."

"Never mind," she said, taking my hand and leading me down the stairs. "Louise is coming too," Sarah announced to her mother.

"Can I, Aunt Kay?"

"Of course, dear."

"Wonderful," Mrs. Hickerson said, smiling. "We'll bring her home this afternoon, Kay. Thank you for the coffee."

"You're very welcome," Aunt Kay said. She held open the door for us. "Have fun, girls."

Mrs. Hickerson's car was a big white Buick. We all sat in the front seat, with Sarah in the middle. The cherry air freshener hanging from the rearview mirror made the car smell sticky-sweet.

When we drove onto the highway Mrs. Hickerson asked, "What church do you and your father belong to?"

"We don't go to church a lot."

No one said anything for a while. Sarah bumped me with her leg and we glanced at each other out of the corners of our eyes. I could see a smile spreading on her face. Mrs. Hickerson cleared her throat. "Your Aunt Kay tells me your father is abroad, doing research."

"Yes, he writes articles for *National Geographic*," I said, even though it was his first for the big magazine.

"How fascinating. Perhaps I will get to read one of them."

"Sure."

I saw a dead raccoon in the road. No one would move the body; it would be there until rain and sun and tires turned it into shreds of skin and fragments of bone. Then I saw a huge cross attached to a strange building that seemed to be growing out of the ground like a giant gourd.

"That's our church," Sarah said.

Mrs. Hickerson drove the Buick into a parking lot. Other people were getting out of cars and walking toward the church in a kind of slow-moving stream, and we joined them. I got a little nervous because people were looking at me and smiling as if I were someone special. I wanted to ask Sarah about it, but no one was talking. Sarah took my hand for the second time. We followed her mother into the church and down an aisle with rows of benches on both sides. Mrs. Hickerson stopped and motioned for me to take a seat. Sarah let go of my hand and sat down on the bench beside me.

Up on stage stood a podium with a microphone sticking up and a small light attached. Behind that stood the giant cross I'd seen from the road, set in a window of frosted glass that made up the whole wall. Mrs. Hickerson said that the church was God's house, but the flowers around the cross weren't real. We folded our hands in our laps and waited. Sarah took a Bible out of the bench in front of us and flipped through the pages so they fanned us. Mrs. Hickerson cleared her throat. Sarah put the Bible back, clasped her hands together, and circled one thumb with the other, round and round.

The minister walked in and Sarah sat up stiff and straight like all the adults, but her face turned pink. I could tell that she was trying not to laugh. The minister stood at the podium and opened a book. He didn't smile at the audience; he just started talking, and he didn't sound very friendly. Soon his face was red and he got louder and louder until it seemed like he might explode. I looked around at the people watching and listening.

The ceiling was so high I wondered how anyone could get up there and clean it or change a light bulb. I thought about the dead raccoon on the road. Back home Dad kept a shovel in the back of the truck. Sometimes he used it to move dead animals off the road. He said that scavengers come to feed on the carcasses, and then they get hit. I wondered if the dead raccoon was a mom with babies waiting in a tree somewhere.

Sarah reached down for a pen that was on the floor under the bench in front of us. It was one of those pens with a button on the end to push and it clicked and the point popped out. Sarah started clicking the pen with her thumb. Her mother patted her on the leg and she stopped and tipped her chin up just a little and made her face smooth and angelic. She tapped my foot with hers and sucked in her cheeks, making a fish face. I did the same to keep from laughing.

I was so relieved when the minister stopped talking and everyone stood up, making just enough commotion for Sarah and me to let out our laughter. Mrs. Hickerson gave Sarah a look. The minister told us to open our psalm books, but he didn't give a page number. Sarah knew where to turn and she held her book out for us to share. The organ player started up and Sarah pretended to sing like an opera singer, but not quite loud enough for her mother to complain. I felt my face get hot and I had to cover my mouth with my hand, which nearly made Sarah crack up. She had to hide her face with the psalm book.

"Sarah," her mother said.

Sarah let the book slide down off her face, which was totally pink but calm. Finally church was over.

When we got in the car Mrs. Hickerson said, "Sarah, I don't know what got into you today."

"It was a nice sermon," Sarah said.

"Smart-aleck," her mother said back.

Sarah tipped up her chin and made her angelic face. I had a lot of questions, but I didn't want to ask with Mrs. Hickerson there.

"How far away do you live?" I asked after a while.

"Across Eighty-sixth Street, just four houses down the block," Sarah said. "Come over tomorrow!"

"Sarah," her mother said, "remember, you have a doctor's appointment tomorrow. Then you have your chores to think of, and packing for Illinois."

"I know, Mom."

"You're going to Illinois?"

"Yeah, my grandma lives there."

"How long will you be gone?"

"A week."

"Here we are, Louise." Mrs. Hickerson put on the turn signal and drove the Buick into Creekside Court.

Sarah grabbed my hand and took the pen she'd found in church and wrote her phone number on my palm. "Call me later."

Aunt Kay was fixing dinner when I walked in. "Did you have a nice time?"

"Uh-huh. Church is weird, but I really like Sarah." I held up my hand with the phone number. "She asked me to call her."

"Well, that's marvelous."

After dinner I took the phone out on the patio and sat down on one of the benches. The air felt warm and it was still light out. A lawn mower buzzed in the distance and a lone robin sang. Back home at dusk I could feel the temperature drop. Cool air would move in and bring the sweet, stony smell of lake water. The phoebe would say, *Phoebe! Phoebe!* until dark, and then frogs would start peeping and clicking and the barred owl would call out, *Oo-oo-oo-OOAAH!*

I read Sarah's number off my hand and pressed the lighted buttons on the phone. It rang on the other end, and I cleared my throat. Her mother answered.

"Mrs. Hickerson, it's Louise. Can I please talk to Sarah?"

"Hello, Louise. Just a moment."

I heard footsteps and pictured Sarah's mom walking down a hallway to Sarah's room. I heard Mrs. Hickerson say, "It's Louise. Don't stay on too long. You need to get ready for bed."

"Hi!" Sarah said.

"Hi," I said back. "Why do you have to go to the doctor?"

"I'm anemic. I have to get another blood test."

"Is that why you have to go to bed early?"

"Yeah, I'm supposed to get lots of rest."

"So you're going away for a week."

"Yeah, my grandma's getting old. Mom says we have to visit more often. What are you doing tomorrow?"

"I don't know. I'll probably go to the place where I found the baby raccoon. You want to come over after the doctor's? I'll show you where I found him."

"I have chores. But you could come here and help me make a dessert for my grandma."

"Okay. How do I get there?"

"You cross Eighty-sixth Street and look for a blue house with a swing on the porch."

No-Bake Desserts

"Are you sure you don't want me to drive you?" Aunt Kay asked.

"It's only a mile."

"You be careful crossing Eighty-sixth Street."

"I will, Aunt Kay."

She gave me a hug. "I know you will, dear. I know you're a big girl, but I can't help but fret. You be sure and call if you need a ride home. Do you know our number?"

"I think so."

"Aha!" she said, tearing off a sheet from her pad. She put on her glasses, wrote down the number, and gave me the paper. I folded it and put it in my pocket and started out for Sarah's house.

I walked past the golf course, past another development like Creekside Court. I had to keep going back and forth across the street because there was only a dirt path and in some places the fencing was so close to the road there wasn't any room. But when I got near Eighty-sixth Street a narrow sidewalk appeared and went all the way to the traffic light. Cars went speeding by in six lanes. McDonald's was on my right, a Mobil station on my left, and the Kroger supermarket beyond. As far as I could see in both directions there were more gas stations and fast-food places.

After I crossed Eighty-sixth Street, everything changed. I was in a neighborhood with tall trees and wide sidewalks on both sides of the street. The houses were small and close together. I saw a swing set in someone's yard and toys strewn around. A bunch of kids were riding bikes right up the middle of the street.

I found the blue house with the swing on the porch and

climbed the steps. The screen door swung open. "Hi!" Sarah said. "I did everything on my list except the dessert. Come on!"

"Where's your mom?"

"Running errands. She won't be back for an hour."

I followed Sarah through the living room. A fan whirred in the corner, and there was a vase of silk flowers surrounded by angel statues on a little table. Round crocheted things lay on the arms of the couch, and on the wall was a picture of Jesus, with eyes that seemed to be looking right at me.

In the kitchen, bowls and measuring cups and spoons were lined up on the counter with a sheet of paper next to them.

"It's a no-bake dessert," Sarah said. "Mom picked out the recipe 'cause it's too hot today to use the oven. You must be dying of thirst. I'll fix lemonade."

I looked at the sheet of paper. The handwriting was cursive and perfectly neat, the opposite of my dad's. "Is this your list?"

"Uh-huh."

I read the list out loud. "'Fold laundry. Sweep floor. Clean bathroom. Pack for Illinois. Make dessert for Grandma.'"

Sarah handed me a glass of lemonade and I took a big drink and said, "Thanks."

She opened the cabinet and took down a box of graham crackers and a bag of sugar and three cans of blueberries.

"Why does your mom give you a list?" I asked.

Sarah rolled her eyes. "Habit. When I was little I forgot stuff. She hasn't figured out that I grew up." She unwrapped two sticks of margarine and dropped them in the bowl. "Start mashing those."

I went to work on the margarine, smashing it against the side of the bowl with the back of the wooden spoon. "Your mom's a teacher, huh?"

"Yes, can't you tell? She's always talking to you like there's a lesson to be learned."

"I thought it was a church thing."

"Maybe that, too." Sarah emptied a cup of sugar into the bowl, and then she ground the graham crackers in a food processor and dumped them in. "Keep mashing."

She went to the refrigerator and took out Cool Whip, cream cheese, and sour cream. She dumped the stuff out of the containers into a bowl with more sugar and mixed it all up with an electric mixer.

"Almost done," she said.

We pressed the graham cracker mix into a rectangular Pyrex baking dish and spread the Cool Whip mixture on. Then Sarah opened the cans of blueberries. The berries were in a thick sauce. She spread them on top and covered the dish with plastic wrap. "Could you get the door?"

I held open the refrigerator door while Sarah put the dessert inside. "Your grandma's going to eat that whole thing?"

"Yep. She loves sweets. Let's go back to my room. But I don't have a TV or anything. Mom thinks it's a bad influence."

"My dad would agree on that. We don't have one either, not at my real home at Marl Lake. Sometimes we watch movies on his computer, though."

"My mom doesn't let me do that. She only lets me go to the movies with the youth group from church."

"That could be fun."

"I guess."

Sarah's room was the same size as mine back home. But the walls and floor and everything were different, all pale pink and fluffy. Even the lampshade was frilly. What Sarah did have that I had were lots of books, mostly religious ones, but also *The Black Stallion* and *The Secret Garden*. Then I saw something on the shelf above the books. It was a bird's nest made out of twigs and dry grass.

"My dad gave that to me." She took it down and put it in my hands. "He and Mom got divorced when I was three."

"Oh. Sorry."

"It's okay. Look inside."

Strands of red hair were woven into the nest. "This looks like your hair," I said.

"It is. Dad snipped some off and hung it out on a bush. Birds came and took it for their nest, and Dad found it in November after the leaves fell off the trees."

"It's really neat." I'd never heard of birds doing that. I knew chipping sparrows would fly a mile to find horsehair for their nests, but I didn't know about a bird using human hair. "Your dad must know a lot about birds."

"He does. He lives out in the country, about an hour from here."

"So you get to see him?"

"Sure, every other weekend. He picks me up and we do a cookout in the park or go to the mall and have ice cream at Farrell's. Sometimes we go arrowhead hunting in the cornfield behind his house or do target practice."

"Target practice?"

"Yeah, my mom doesn't like it, but too bad."

Outside, a car door slammed. "Sarah? Come help with the groceries, please."

Sarah and I each carried in a bag of groceries from the car. "Thank you, girls," Mrs. Hickerson said. "Louise, can I give you a ride home?"

"No, thank you. I like to walk."

"I'll walk with you part of the way," Sarah said.

"Sarah, have you packed?"

"Oops. Just to the end of the block, Mom."

Mrs. Hickerson sighed. "And come right back."

Sarah and I hopped down the steps two at a time and then we walked as slow as we could.

"Where is Marl Lake?" Sarah asked.

I held up my hand like a mitten and pointed to the middle knuckle on my middle finger. The mitten was Michigan, sticking up between two of the Great Lakes.

"My dad took me sailing once, up on Lake Michigan."

"Really? Did you like it?"

"Uh-huh, especially the fudge they make."

"That's for tourists."

"Maybe, but it sure is good. Wish I had some right now."

"Yeah, me too. The milk chocolate kind, with pecans. Hey, you could come visit me at Marl Lake."

"My mom won't drive me that far."

"I know there's a bus. My dad will pick you up at the station."

"She'll never let me do that."

We reached the end of Sarah's block and stood on the corner under the traffic light.

"Thanks for helping make dessert."

"Sure, that was fun. I never heard of a no-bake dessert before. Except pudding. But even that, you have to cook."

"You never made zebra cake?"

"No. What's that?"

"It's easy. You get these chocolate cookies. They're thin and crisp and you spread Cool Whip all over each one and stack them up and then cover the whole thing with Cool Whip. You put it in the fridge over night and the cookies puff up and you've got cake."

"Is it good?"

"The best! I'll make it for you."

"So you're gone a whole week."

"I'll call as soon as I get back."

I reached in my pocket and pulled out the piece of paper Aunt Kay wrote the phone number on and gave it to Sarah.

"Thanks. I better go."

"Okay. Bye."

The light changed and I crossed Eighty-sixth Street. When I got to the other side I turned. Sarah had turned too; she waved and I waved back. I could find things to do for a week and then she'd be home. Maybe I'd let Aunt Kay show me how to sew something after all.

My Own Private Church

When I got home Aunt Kay and Uncle Jack were sitting in the living room. I looked at them looking at me. "What?"

Aunt Kay stood up and came to me and put her arms around me.

"What happened? Is my dad okay?"

"Yes, but your cat has been hit by a car, dear. He's dead."

"No, Cash is fine. He's home and the Lees are looking after him."

"Mrs. Lee called this afternoon. They hadn't seen Cash in a week or so and then one of the boys found him on the road, about two miles from the cottage."

"Then it's a different cat. How could he be so far from home?"

Aunt Kay stroked my hair and looked into my eyes. "Dear, it was Cash. Mr. Lee buried him behind your garden, near the woods."

"No," I said again. Then I quit talking. My legs were so heavy. Tears trickled down my cheeks. Uncle Jack stood up and pulled a handkerchief from his pocket and came and gently wiped my face. The handkerchief smelled like clean, dry grass, the way the baby rabbit did.

"I want to lie down," I said.

Aunt Kay and Uncle Jack didn't say anything. I went upstairs to my room and shut the door. I lay down on the bed and my eyes and nose ran, making a wet patch on the pillow. Inside my head I saw Cash's green eyes watching us drive away. I made fists with my hands that would never pet his silky fur. I punched the pillow. I was so angry at my dad for going away and making me be here instead of home, where I should have been. Cash had left the cottage to try to find me. I thought about him out there, lost and afraid and getting run over, and I rubbed his collar against my face and cried.

Later that night Aunt Kay brought tomato soup and crackers and cheese up on a tray and left it on the bedside table. I pretended to be asleep.

When it got dark and the house was finally quiet I got out of bed and dragged a chair over to the window. Carefully I pulled the lever to unlock it and cranked the handle until the window opened. A nighttime breeze soothed my swollen face. The air conditioner came on and I got up and shut the vents and turned up the thermostat on the wall to eighty degrees. I sat back down in the chair and looked out at the stars.

I remembered the time I yelled at Cash for bringing in a cardinal. "Get out of here, you!" I'd shouted, holding the red bird's torn-up body in my hand. "He can't help it, Lews," Dad had said.

I knew Dad was right. How I wished I could take it back, the mean way I shouted at Cash and glared at him. I squeezed my eyes shut because it hurt so much to think of how he crept off when I yelled at him. I'd give anything to make Cash know how much I loved him and how much I missed him. I held his collar on my wrist. Down in the yard a cricket chirped. A few of Uncle Jack's white roses had opened. I could see them in the dark, like a cluster of pale ghost faces.

In the morning it was quiet. No mower, no washing machine. Not even birds. I remembered about Cash and my eyes filled up and I lay there with my head on the pillow and tears running down into my hair and my ears. I tried to imagine, was it quick for him, like with my cousin Penny? Maybe Cash didn't know what hit him. Maybe in an instant he was gone. If that was true, I was the only one to suffer.

After a while I looked over at my tortoise necklace on the bedside table. Next to it was the tray with the soup and crackers from last night. I still felt mad at my dad. I wished I could talk to him—he'd say something to make even this better. He would feel terrible if he knew what had happened. One time when Cash was still a kitten, just a tiny ball of fur with ears and a tail, I walked into the room and Dad was asleep in his chair with Cash in his lap. I tiptoed over to get my kitten and Dad opened one eye and said, "Leave the kitty be." I tiptoed back out of the room, feeling happy that Dad shared my love for Cash.

Aunt Kay tapped on the door and poked her head in. "Feeling okay, dear?"

"I guess so. I wish I could talk to my dad."

"I don't know if we can reach him directly. But maybe we can leave a message with the *Geographic* office. Shall we try?"

Downstairs in the kitchen Aunt Kay took out the number Dad left in case of an emergency. She punched in the number. After being transferred a couple times Aunt Kay got hold of the right person and gave me the phone.

"Hello?" I said. "Jeff Eliot is my dad and he's in Brazil now, writing your article. And I need to leave him a message that my cat got run over by a car."

"Oh, I am sorry, honey. What was your cat's name?"

"Cash."

"I'll be sure your father gets your message the next time the team checks in."

I said thank you and hung up the phone.

"Okay?" Aunt Kay asked.

I nodded my head yes.

"Now, how about breakfast? I'll fix up some nice scrambled eggs and cinnamon toast."

Aunt Kay and Uncle Jack tried extra hard to make me feel better. A couple of nights Uncle Jack drove us up Eighty-sixth Street to the

Ben and Jerry's for hot fudge sundaes. Aunt Kay made popcorn in the microwave and brought it upstairs and watched movies with me. That week, I ate more ice cream and cake and popcorn than ever. And chocolate-covered peanuts from the candy jar. Uncle Jack would say, "How about you and me playing a game of checkers?"

We'd sit down at the card table in the living room and put our checkers in place on the board. I got to be red. I'd wait for Uncle Jack to say, "Reach in that jar and get us each some candy," which he did every time, sooner or later. He didn't let me beat him at checkers, though, not once.

I still went to listen for the other baby raccoon even though I knew he'd been dead a long time. I sat down on the rocks I'd stacked and leaned against the tree and I looked at the big, hollow branch that reached into the sky. The raccoon's body was up there, all cleaned out by bugs. Mice would gnaw on the cartilage and bones and his skeleton would fall apart and after a while he would become part of the rotting wood in that old branch. Sitting under the tree, I thought that that place was my own private church. Instead of thinking about how Cash died and how he might have suffered, I tried to imagine him being with the baby raccoon somewhere, playing around and getting into mischief.

ANIMAL SOULS

Aunt Kay and I were decorating an angel food cake, making flowers out of sliced strawberries and white icing, when Sarah finally called. "We're back. What'd you do all week?"

"Cash got hit by a car and he's dead."

"No way, that's terrible. Mom!" Sarah yelled. "Louise's cat got killed. Drive me over there?"

I could hear Mrs. Hickerson saying something in the background.

"Yes, now!" Sarah hollered. Then to me she said, "I'll be there in half an hour."

The white Buick pulled up in front. Sarah got out, said something to her mother, put a small backpack over her shoulder, and shut the car door. Mrs. Hickerson waved and drove off.

Sarah hurried up the steps and wrapped her arms around me. "Poor Louise," she said.

My throat tightened and I hugged her back. "How long can you stay?"

"Until supper."

"Want to go see where I found the baby raccoon?"

"Yeah."

"Let's get water."

We went inside and I wrote a note for Aunt Kay, telling her what we were up to. I took two bottles of water from the fridge and we started out.

Sarah unzipped her backpack so I could put the water bottles in. She took out a baggie of raisins and peanuts. "Want some?"

I took a few raisins and chewed them slowly. They stuck to my teeth and made me thirsty. "Wait, now I need the water."

Sarah held the backpack open and I got out a bottle and took a drink.

"Thanks," I said, zipping up the pack. "How's your grandma?"

"She's fine. Getting old. She says thanks, by the way."

"For what?"

"Helping make the dessert."

"You told her about me?"

"Yeah, all about my new friend with the *National Geographic* writer for a dad."

"It's his first article for them."

"So? He's famous as far as Grandma's concerned. Does your dad know about Cash?"

"I left a message."

"My grandma has a cat. She'd probably die if something happened to it. Seriously, that cat's the only company she's got these days."

"What's his name?"

"Scarlett. She's got orange fur."

"It didn't bother you, being in the same house with a cat?"

"I sneezed and itched and Mom gave me an antihistamine. Will you get another cat?"

"I don't know."

"Too soon to even think about it, huh. I shouldn't have asked."

"No, it's okay. I can't replace Cash. But if someone handed me a kitten right now I wouldn't say no."

We came to the end of the sidewalk where the path into the trees began. A monarch butterfly flew in front of us, dipping down and fluttering up, and we followed him into the empty lot. It was being taken over by weeds and starting to look like a field. The monarch fluttered around milkweed stalks and we watched him drink nectar from the purple flowers. When he flew to the next cluster of milkweed, he was surprisingly fast, leading us farther across the field.

Yellow and white flowers, daisies and yarrow, bloomed around us, and different kinds of bees buzzed from one flower to another, collecting nectar. The fat bumblebees made the stalks dip and bob. One of the bumblebees didn't look right. He hung from a white yarrow flower at a funny angle.

"Look," I said. "A crab spider."

The spider was white with pink stripes on the sides of her body, which was round as a pearl. She was only half the size of the bee, but she held him steady with her four long front legs. The other four legs were short, and the spider held on to the flower with them. The bee's fuzzy legs were covered with yellow powdery pollen from all the flowers he had visited.

Sarah leaned in to see. "A white spider! I never saw one before. She's eating the bee?"

"Uh-huh. She doesn't make a web like other spiders. She's camouflaged and she waits for bugs to come to the flower."

"All spiders are girls?"

"No, but it's the females you see most of the time. They're bigger and fatter. See how fat she is? She must be close to making her egg sac."

Sarah giggled. "How do you know about bugs?"

"I just look at them a lot. Back home I usually find crab spiders in the goldenrod, and they're yellow, because goldenrod is yellow."

"When they're born do they see what color they are and then know what color flower to hide in?"

"I don't know. I know she can see us when we move. One time I swatted a deer fly and stuck him on the end of a blade of grass and held him out to a crab spider. I could see her watching and moving her body to follow the fly, and then suddenly she grabbed him. Jumping spiders will do the same thing."

Sarah tilted her head to one side. "She's pretty."

"I think so too."

I saw a big scrap of asphalt roofing a little way off. Weeds had pushed up one corner, but most of it was so settled on the ground that I figured it must have been left over from when Creekside Court was built.

"Sarah, look." I squatted and lifted the corner and flipped over the roofing. Black crickets scattered, and a grass spider big as a silver dollar, with a marble-sized egg sac, seemed to fly over the grass. There was a ball of dried leaves that was probably the nest of a field mouse. A little orange centipede scurried away. Stuck to the corner of the roofing was a small wasp nest on a stalk the size of a toothpick. A wasp circled us.

"Don't swat at him, just keep still," I told Sarah.

She nodded and watched the wasp. He settled on the nest, his wings and antennae twitching nervously.

"See how they make their nest?" I said. "The rows are all in different shades of gray."

Sarah squatted down close to me and studied the nest. "They make paper. How do they do that?"

"By chewing up dead wood and spitting it out in those rows. They shape the wet pulp with their jaws and legs. I think there's something in their spit that glues it all together."

Sarah ducked her head as another wasp circled and landed on the nest. "Wow, it's a whole neighborhood under there."

"Yeah. We should turn it over again so they can have their houses back."

We stood up and saw the monarch way across the field. Sarah said, "Let's look around and see if there's more stuff to turn over."

We found a cardboard box, all flattened out and heavy with moisture. I squatted and took a corner in my hand. "Ready?"

Sarah nodded.

I turned over the cardboard. Again, bugs of all kinds scattered. And there in a coil was a little rusty-brown DeKay snake. Right away I cupped my hand over him and picked him up.

Sarah jumped back. "I'm scared of snakes."

"Don't be. Especially these. Look." I opened my hand so she could see the snake. He was so little he fit in my palm. He kept himself in a tight coil, hiding his head, which was no bigger than the tip of my pinkie finger. "He couldn't hurt you even if he wanted to, and he doesn't want to, he just wants to be put back down."

Sarah leaned in a little, looking at the snake.

"Now, look at this." I slipped my finger under the snake and turned him over.

Sarah took in a breath. "He's orange!"

The snake righted himself, and I cupped my hand over him so he'd stay calm. "Wanna hold him?"

"I don't know," Sarah said, putting her hands in her pockets.

"Didn't you ever hold a snake?"

She shook her head.

"Look how little he is! This could be your big chance." I opened my hands. The coil of his body was not much thicker than a shoelace. He flicked out his tongue so fast it was hard to see. His chin was white with gray specks and his eyes were like tiny beads. Lightly I stroked his smooth, rusty brown back.

Sarah held very still, looking at the snake. "Okay," she said finally, sucking in air. She rubbed her hands together and then held them out. I took one by the wrist and tipped my hand with the snake slowly to let the snake roll into her palm. She made a little gasp and her shoulders went up. I kept a hold on her wrist so the snake wouldn't fall if Sarah panicked. But she stared at the small brown snake in her hand. She touched his back with a finger. Her shoulders relaxed. She smiled. "He's soft."

"Uh-huh." I let go of her wrist.

Sarah petted the snake lightly. He uncoiled himself in her hand and moved his head, flicking his tongue in and out.

Sarah let out a small laugh. "He's cute!" She watched the snake move across her hand. She put her finger in front of him and he climbed over it. She laughed again and looked up at me.

I turned the cardboard back over. "Wanna let him go soon?"

"I should, huh." Sarah knelt and put her hand beside the box. Flicking his tongue in and out, the snake moved toward the edge of the cardboard and then, moving quickly, he slipped out of Sarah's hand. "Wait till I tell my dad I held a snake!" Sarah stood up, her eyes big. "He's picking me up this weekend. You could come with us!"

"Really?"

"Of course!"

A grasshopper clicked his wings and leapt up in the air and flew across the field a little way before coming down in the weeds.

"Let's go look at that tree where you found the raccoon."

We made it through the briars, holding thorny branches aside for each other. Sarah stood on the rocks I'd stacked and looked in the hole. "Nothing in here. So, you think the other one's dead?"

"For sure. He was so little he could never have survived without his mother."

"That's sad." Sarah stepped down, brushing off her hands. We stood for a moment, both of us looking up into the leafy branches of the big tree.

"I like to imagine him and Cash playing together somewhere," I said.

"That would be nice, if animals went to heaven."

"They do."

"That's not what the Bible says."

"Well, if there aren't any animals in heaven, I'm not going."

"Louise, you don't want to go to hell."

"I do if Cash is there."

"He's not. Animals don't go anyplace when they die."

I shrugged. I was afraid to tell Sarah that I didn't believe in heaven or hell. "You believe in God?"

"Don't you?"

"I don't know. Not the way that minister says I'm supposed to."

"He's an airbag." She covered her mouth. "Don't tell anyone I said that."

"I won't. But you think God is a bearded man in the clouds?"

"I don't know if God has a beard. Jesus does."

"But where do they live?"

"Everywhere."

"How can that be?"

"God is a holy spirit. He lives in each of us."

"Oh. What about the crab spider? Does God live inside animals that small?"

"He doesn't, because animals don't have souls."

"Yes they do."

"How do you know?"

"I just do. Besides, if I have one, so does every other animal."

Sarah looked up at the hole in the tree. "You miss Cash a lot, huh?"

"Yeah."

"My dad has a dog. You'll like him, his name's Buster. We'll do something fun Saturday."

NEWT AND THE BUTTERFLIES

I sat in the chair by the window, pulling Cash's collar around and around my wrist. By the clock on the fireplace mantel, Sarah and her dad were almost five minutes late. I was trying to focus on the thought of a whole day with Sarah, trying to forget the awful pictures of Cash walking along the road, lost and meowing, looking for me and then getting run over and lying on the road, bleeding, not dead yet. I squeezed my eyes shut and rubbed them with my fists. I told myself that maybe it wasn't bad like that. Would I rather not know how he died so I wouldn't have the pictures? Would it be better if he had just disappeared? Maybe then I'd be wondering if coyotes got him, or an owl. I'd heard of great horned owls taking cats.

A blue pickup truck stopped in front of the house. HICKERSON CONSTRUCTION was printed on the door in black letters.

"Aunt Kay, they're here!" I yelled, jumping out of my chair. I pulled open the door before Sarah could ring the doorbell, and we both said "Hi!" at the same time.

Sarah's red hair was in braids, which made her freckles show more.

Aunt Kay came out of the kitchen. "Have fun, girls."

I ran down the steps and hopped into the truck after Sarah. A dog landed in my lap, panting and sniffing my face.

"Meet Buster," Sarah's dad said. He had blue eyes like Sarah's and a beard with red in it, the same color as Sarah's hair. "He's real friendly. And you can call me Newt."

Buster started licking my face when I tried to tell Newt my

name. I put my arms around Buster and wiped my face on his brindled coat. I smelled his doggy smell.

"Settle down, boy," Newt said.

Buster obeyed, dropping himself right across our laps. His tail whapped Newt's leg and his front half rested on mine, with Sarah getting the middle part. Buster looked up at me with his brown eyes and I petted his floppy ears. The weight of him on my lap felt good. "I'm Louise," I said.

"Pleased to meet you," Newt said, putting the truck in gear. He drove out of Creekside Court and down the road to Eighty-sixth Street.

Sarah nudged me with her elbow, just to say how excited she was. I nudged her back. It felt good to be out, riding in the truck. There was a gun rack behind my head like the one in my dad's Park Service truck.

"Sarah tells me she held a snake you girls found."

"Yes, a little DeKay snake, out in that field past Creekside Court."

"He wasn't so little," Sarah said.

I nudged her with my elbow. "You were very brave."

From the corner of my eye I could see Newt grinning. "After lunch," he said, "I thought we might see the butterfly exhibit at the zoo. What do you girls say?"

"Yay, Dad! Can we get burritos?"

"You bet. Okay by you, Louise?"

"I love butterflies. And burritos."

Newt put on the turn signal and merged into traffic on the highway. "Sarah told me about your cat too. I'm awful sorry."

"Thank you," I said. "This is his collar." I held up my wrist to show Newt.

He smiled. "That's a fine bracelet. How long did you have him for?"

"Since he was a kitten. My dad gave him to me for my sixth birthday."

"You had him about half your life, then, if I guess your age correctly."

"Uh-huh."

"That's a terrible loss. Animals give us something special, don't they? Something people can't."

"It's true," I said.

"I bet you have a lot of good memories."

"I do." I remembered when Cash was still a kitten. Whenever he got scared his fur would stick straight out and he would come tearing across the room and climb up my leg. I felt his tiny needle claws through my jeans. I'd gather him in my arms and hold him until he quit being scared.

"But I can't get rid of the terrible pictures," I said. Buster watched me, his ears forward. I rested my hand on his head. "I see Cash lying on the road, broken and hurting."

"They won't go away," Newt said. "But you'll stop having them all the time. The good times you remember will start to squeeze out the bad pictures. That's one of the nice things about how memory works."

I was glad Newt didn't tell me to just stop thinking about it, or that it was quick and that surely Cash didn't suffer. Because he did or he didn't and I will never know. Cash got killed by a car and it was terrible. It was also over. Whether he suffered or not, it was in the past. He wasn't suffering now. I wanted to keep thinking about it that way.

We went to the drive-through at a Taco Bell and got burritos and then we headed for the zoo. Newt parked the truck in the shade of a maple tree, and we took our lunch out to one of the picnic tables.

"Stay close," Newt told Buster. The dog sat down and waited for scraps of our tortillas.

"I understand your father's down in Brazil, writing an article," Newt said.

"Uh-huh, about the rain forest and jaguars. He's supposed to write about the trip he's on with these biologists and the animals they find along the way."

"That sounds like one of the most fascinating things a person could do. He's lucky to have work like that."

"Yeah, he was pretty excited when he got the job." I wished I had worn my tortoise necklace so I could show Newt.

After lunch Newt opened the truck door. "Come on, boy."

Buster jumped up and sat down on the seat, ears forward, eyes on Newt.

"Watch the truck," Newt said to him, rolling the windows down partway.

Going into the butterfly exhibit was like stepping inside a giant terrarium, thick with ferns and moss and leafy vines hanging down. Butterflies were everywhere, all around us. I never saw so many different sizes and shapes and colors before. Orange and black, yellow, white, pink, even bright green butterflies fluttered high and low, alighting on the broad, shiny leaves of tropical plants. Sunlight came in through the glass ceiling and walls and the air was moist and sweet-smelling. Part of the sweet smell came from cut oranges and feeders full of nectar put up for the butterflies.

Dazzled by the fluttering and colors of wings we grew quiet and drifted in different directions. I saw an orange butterfly the color of melon and another, smaller, with black-and-yellow-striped wings. Another was pure white with tiny black spots, and the edges of his wings were deckled. I thought he looked like flying lace. A butterfly with spots like big eyes lit on my hand and I held my breath. I kept quiet, even though I wanted to call out to Sarah. The butterfly walked up my arm while he opened and shut his wings, showing the purple-black color on the tops of them. I saw his antennae and his round eyes like great big poppy seeds. Suddenly he flapped his wings and flew above my head and landed on a fern.

I turned and saw another butterfly, this one sitting on a leaf with his brown wings folded. He opened them and I caught my breath. The tops of his wings were blue and shimmering and I knew that he was a blue morpho, like the butterfly in my poster from Brazil. My dad was seeing blue morphos, maybe at that very moment. I wished I could hold the butterfly and I wanted to put out my hand so he might climb onto me, but I remembered the sign at the door, *Please Do Not Touch.*

I heard Newt calling for us to come look at something. He stood in front of a box mounted on a post. The box had a glass front and inside there were rods going across, with chrysalises attached, like the monarch makes, only different sizes and colors.

"Look, girls," Newt said. "One is just coming out."

Sarah and I watched as the butterfly slowly pulled out his legs and finally his antennae. He clung to the chrysalis upside down, his shriveled wings under his swollen body.

"See the wings?" Newt said. "The butterfly's heart will pump fluid into them until they're completely opened up."

I remembered when I was little, how I had watched a polyphemus moth coming out of his chrysalis. I remembered that I had been upset—I thought something was wrong with the moth because his body was fat and his wings were all crumpled.

"Don't worry, Lews," my dad said. "You just watch. That moth will pump fluid from his body into those wings until they're all spread out."

I looked at Newt, watching the butterfly's wings uncurl. His face was lit up with excitement. "Isn't nature miraculous!"

"Yeah, it is," Sarah said.

When we were done looking at the butterflies I asked Newt, "Do you think we could see if they have a jaguar?"

"Sure we can, Louise. I bet if we make our way over to where they keep the big cats, we'll find one."

Newt was right—they did have a jaguar. But the one they had was all black, no spots. The plaque on the railing said he was hypermelanistic, and that the spots were there but hard to see because of the dark fur in between. He was on loan to the zoo for the summer, and he looked as though he knew it, too—it seemed like he was just waiting to go back home to his rain forest. In the other enclosures the cats were stretched out in the sun, up on the big rocks, or napping in the shade under a tree. But the jaguar paced along the fence of his enclosure. I don't know why, but I put my hands behind my back, hiding Cash's collar. I watched the muscles in the jaguar's shoulders and hindquarters roll as he walked and I tried to imagine what it would be like to meet him in the forest. A few other people stood and watched the jaguar pace. No one was talking. I stared at the jaguar, thinking I could get him to look at me. He looked my way once, but his eyes flickered past mine as if I weren't there.

Late that afternoon, riding home in Newt's truck with Sarah beside me and Buster across our laps, I thought about the black jaguar and how he should go back home and not be in the zoo. Cash paced only when Dad wouldn't open the door for him. Dad would say, "Do I look like the doorman? Go use your cat door, you rascal!"

Dad used to say that whenever I opened the door for Cash I was encouraging his bad habit. I opened it for him anyway. I never could say no to anything Cash wanted. And now that he was dead I was glad I gave him everything while he was alive. I hoped he knew how much I loved him.

My eyes stung and I had to quit thinking about Cash. I felt Buster watching me. We looked at each other and I petted his wrinkled brow and he whapped Newt's leg with his tail. I wondered if Newt believed Buster had a soul.

A ROUTINE OPERATION

Uncle Jack's mower woke me the next morning. He'd been starting extra early to avoid the midsummer heat. He was usually done by breakfast time and then he'd work on his roses. Afternoons he'd spend cooling down in a comfy chair, watching a golf tournament on TV.

I stayed in bed a while and thought about the blue morpho and how I wished I could see one in the wild. I bet if I turned over a piece of asphalt roofing in the rain forest, I would find a whole world of animals I'd never seen before. I was happy that Sarah agreed with her dad about nature being miraculous. I didn't care whether she thought it was God's miracle or a miracle all on its own.

I got out of bed and put on my dress to wear to church. It was all faded and kind of worn out, but I liked it. Then I took my tortoise necklace off the bedside table and put it on and I went downstairs.

"Well, good morning, sunshine," Aunt Kay said. "Don't you look lovely!" She was sitting at the kitchen table looking at a bunch of papers.

"Morning, Aunt Kay. What're you reading?"

"I'm looking at dress patterns. Are you going to church with Sarah this morning?"

"Uh-huh."

"Then we'd better get you some breakfast."

I broke eggs into a bowl while Aunt Kay put two slices of bread in the toaster. The kitchen darkened and I looked out the window and saw that the sky had clouded over.

"Looks like we might get some rain," Aunt Kay said.

The phone rang. I took the spatula and stirred the eggs while Aunt Kay answered. "It's Sarah," she said, handing the phone to me.

"Hello?"

"Louise, my grandma's in the hospital."

"What's wrong?"

"The doctors can't tell exactly. But Mom says you can't come to church with us, 'cause we're leaving right after to go to Illinois."

"All right. I hope your grandma's okay. Will you call me?"

"I'll try. I have to go."

"Okay, bye."

I gave the phone back to Aunt Kay. "Her grandma's in the hospital. I can't go to church because they're leaving for Illinois."

"Oh, that's a shame. I hope it's nothing serious." Aunt Kay put the phone back in the cradle. "I'll make us a nice cup of cocoa."

After breakfast Aunt Kay and I sat at the table drinking our cocoa. I thought it was funny that she made a hot drink when it was ninety degrees outside. It was what she did when things got tough.

"Well," she said, "Jeff will be coming home in a couple of weeks. Are you looking forward to going back to Marl Lake?"

"Yes. When I get there I'll see where Cash is buried."

"Yes you will, dear."

"It will be so different without him. We did everything together, almost." I could feel sadness squeezing my throat shut. Aunt Kay sat perfectly still, watching me over the top of her glasses, listening. "I miss him so much," I said, and then the hot tears were rolling down my face again.

Aunt Kay reached out and put her hand over mine. She listened a hundred percent; she didn't gaze off into space the way my dad always did. We sat like that a minute. I wiped my face on my napkin and took a deep breath.

"I'll miss you and Uncle Jack and Sarah."

"Then I guess you'll have to come visit, won't you?" She patted my hand and smiled. "Would you like to look at some of these patterns? I want to make a dress for you, if you would like that."

"I don't know if I can be much help, but I'll try."

"You don't have to, dear. Not if you don't want to. But I bet you'd like to pick out some fabric. Shall we go downtown this afternoon? It looks like a rainy day, and that's just right for a sewing project."

"Okay," I said. "I really like this." I lifted the worn hem of my dress. The orange, yellow, and violet in the pattern were the colors of sunset on Marl Lake in summertime.

"We can find something very like it," Aunt Kay said.

It stormed and rained all day Sunday and there had been a tornado watch through the night. Monday morning the wind died, but the rain continued. I sat on the floor of the sewing room helping Aunt Kay lay out the fabric for my dress. I'd found a light green cotton with orange and yellow flowers on it. I liked it even more than my old dress.

Uncle Jack yelled up the stairs that the mail had come. Aunt Kay frowned. "He wouldn't do that unless he thought there was something important."

"My dad?"

"Let's go see."

Something had come from Brazil, a letter this time. It had more of those stamps with exotic beetles and spiders and orchids. The postmark was dated a week ago. I sat down at the kitchen table and opened it.

Dear Lews,

I just got your message and I hardly know what to say, except that I am so sorry. I think about what a good friend

Cash was to you and to me and of all the times I watched the two of you head down the path, side by side, on your walks into the woods. I just can't believe he's gone.

Remember the time we watched him with that chipmunk? How he got fooled into believing the chipmunk was hurt and how that little critter pretended to limp in bigger and bigger circles and then he saw his chance and zoom! Gone, into the woodpile. The look on Cash's face! And what was even funnier was how Cash caught the chipmunk again and again that summer, and the chipmunk played the same trick. Cash knew it, didn't he? And he played along. Maybe he knew that if he killed the chipmunk the game would be over.

Louise, honey, until I'm home all I can do is say how sorry I am and that I'm thinking about Cash and about you.

Love,
Dad

I looked up at Aunt Kay.

"Everything all right?" she asked.

"Yes, he's writing about Cash." I folded the letter and put it back in the envelope. "I think I'll take a walk. It looks like the sky is clearing."

The grass was extra green and wet, and earthworms were scattered all over the sidewalk like sticks that had been tossed up in the air and left wherever they fell. Little rivers flooded the gutters along the road, and leaves blown from the trees by the hard wind stuck to the asphalt. Something hopped into the road and I ran to see. A frog sat right in the middle on the yellow lines, and a string of cars was coming too fast for me to get him in time. I stood and held my breath and my heart beat fast and I clenched my fists. *Oh, please, oh, please! Don't run him over. I don't want to see it!* But I couldn't take my eyes off the frog. I gritted my teeth as the cars passed, missing him by inches. I ran out and scooped him up fast and held on tight, because he was slippery as a wet bar of soap. More cars went by, not slowing down at all, but that was fine, I had the frog safe in my hands, and I said, "What were you doing in the middle of the road? You would have been squashed." I carried him back to the house.

Up in my room, I put the frog in the bathtub while I went to get Penny's old fish tank. I dragged a chair over to the closet and got the tank down off the shelf. After washing it out in the sink, I put the frog in and put on the screened top.

"Wait," I told him. "I'll get you something to hide in."

In the garage I found a pottery plant saucer and then I took a handful of mulch from Uncle Jack's roses and I tore off a piece of sod from the edge of the lawn. I put water from the hose in so the sod and wood chips would stay soggy, and I carried the saucer up the stairs, careful not to spill. Slowly I moved the lid aside and set the saucer down inside the tank. The frog could hop in and wriggle down in the sod and mulch to hide and stay wet.

I sat down cross-legged on the floor beside the tank. I watched the frog's sides move with his breathing. He wiped his eye clean with his foot. His throat drummed. He didn't hop into the saucer. I really wanted to hold him some more, so I reached in and cupped my hand over him and lifted him up.

He wriggled and pushed against my fingers, but finally he held still enough for me to get a close look at him. His skin was olive green, with bright, almost metallic green around his eyes. He had dark spots ringed in gold on his back and legs. I bet he came from the pond on the golf course. I knew that I should take him there, but I didn't see what harm it could do to keep him for just one night. When I opened my hand the frog shot through the air and landed on the rug. He made it to the wall in four leaps, where he hopped along the molding as if looking for the way out. He went limp when I picked him up and he didn't move except for his drumming throat. Wool from the rug stuck to his skin, making him sticky and fuzzy. I put him back inside the tank and wetted my finger in the sod and helped him wipe off the woolly stuff, and then I put the lid on and sat back down.

The moment I moved my hand to brush away the hair from my face, the frog jumped straight up and whacked the screen of the lid, making it jump.

"Ow!" I said. "Your poor nose. Why did you do that?"

It was a dumb question. He wanted out. First he jumped and smacked the glass walls. Then he jumped up, hitting the screen again.

He was like the baby wood duck I found once. The tiny duck had been running straight up the road when I saw him, flapping his fuzzy wings and frantically peeping. Dad helped me set up one of my tanks for the baby duck. We kept him overnight—Dad was going to take him the next day to the bird sanctuary, where they kept orphaned or injured birds until they could be released. I'd given him a dish of seeds and grains and a water bowl and a soft towel to nestle in, but the baby duck started jumping straight up again and again, almost bumping his head against the lid. Dad said that was what baby wood ducks did to get out of the nest, which was way up in a tree, inside a hole.

"Mama duck stands on the ground," Dad said, "and she calls up to the babies to come out of the nest. They have to jump straight up and out of the nest hole and drop all the way to the ground. Once they're all out, she leads them to water. But sometimes an egg hatches late and a baby gets left behind."

I thought it was the saddest thing I'd ever heard, and I watched the baby wood duck jumping up and jumping up, trying so hard to get out and find his mom.

Now the frog jumped again and I said, "You want out, don't you?"

I pushed the lid off the tank, caught the frog, and held on to him with both hands as I carried him outside. I walked up the sidewalk to about the same place where he'd been on the road and, looking across into the golf course, I saw the pond.

When there was a gap in the traffic I crossed the road. I jumped over the ditch and climbed the fence. It was easy, even holding the frog, because the fence was only there to make the golf course look like a fancy horse farm, with the white-painted posts and criss-crossed railing. Still, I knew that I wasn't supposed to be there and I hurried to the pond. I could see a few golf balls on the bottom, like sunken turtle eggs. Fat tadpoles wriggled along the muddy bottom.

"This has got to be where you came from," I said to the frog. Then I lowered him into the water and opened my hands. He waited a second, and then with one kick of his legs he was gone, down under the water.

I didn't wait around to see where he came up—I just wanted to get out of the golf course before someone saw me. I climbed over the fence and ran across the road and all the way back to the house.

Aunt Kay had made us cocoa. "Come sit," she said. "There's been a call from the *National Geographic* office. Your dad's appendix. It had to come out."

"Is he okay? Where is he?"

"In the hospital, dear. They lifted him out in a helicopter. He's going to be fine. The surgery went very well. Just a slight infection, and they want to keep him for a day or two."

"Is he still coming home in two weeks?"

"The nice lady from the office didn't say otherwise."

"Can I talk to him?"

"Not just yet, dear. But don't you worry, now. An appendectomy is a routine operation."

I knew it was sort of common and I'd never heard of anyone dying from appendicitis before. Then I thought, *Maybe Dad will come home sooner, since he probably can't go back to work in the rain forest.* "I hope he finished his article," I said.

Aunt Kay put her hands around her mug of cocoa. "I can't wait to see it when the magazine comes out. God bless him for persevering with his writing."

I looked at my Aunt Kay. She'd said she didn't believe in God the way Sarah and her mom did.

"Do you think that animals have souls?" I asked.

Aunt Kay sat back in her chair. "Hmm. I haven't really thought about it. I mean, it hasn't occurred to me as something to think about." She frowned. "You know, it's been quite a while since I've even had contact with an animal." Then she kind of laughed. "That baby raccoon you found was as close as I've come in so long. Well, my goodness." Aunt Kay's eyelids fluttered and she wiped her eyes with her napkin.

Right then I had the urge to hug my Aunt Kay. But I kept still and listened to her the way she listened to me.

"I gave up on ever having them in my life when my dad took away that little gray kitten," she said. She shrugged her shoulders and blinked as if pushing aside the memory.

"Hey," I said, "what if we go upstairs and have a look at my dress pattern?"

ONLY THE BUZZ OF CICADAS

I wondered what our crows were up to on Marl Lake. This year's babies would be long gone from the nest, but they'd still be getting food from mom and dad. Baby crow voices took a while to mature and when they cried for food it almost sounded like a human baby going, *Aaah! Aaah!* It was so funny to hear their cries being stifled by mom or dad stuffing food down their throats. I hoped the crows would be there when we got home, and maybe if we really were going home sooner, they would be.

Sarah stayed in Illinois through the weekend and by midweek I started to think that if she didn't come back soon I might not get to say goodbye. But she called that night. "My grandma's okay. We brought her home Monday and helped her settle in."

"Thank goodness. Now my dad's in the hospital."

"What happened?"

"Appendicitis. They lifted him out in a helicopter."

"Wow! But that's nothing to worry about. A lot of people get appendicitis."

"I'm not really worried. He's supposed to get out any day now."

"Can you still come with us Saturday?"

"Definitely. What time?"

"Same as before, ten o'clock."

Saturday morning Newt's blue pickup truck made a turn into our cul-de-sac and I headed for the door, yelling, "Bye, Aunt Kay!"

I nearly crashed into Uncle Jack, coming in with the morning paper. "Whoops!" he said, catching me. "Hold on, hold on." He reached into his pocket. "You might need a little money, now." He put a ten-dollar bill in my hand. "Have fun, kiddo."

"Thanks, Uncle Jack!" I ran down the steps and climbed into the truck beside Sarah.

"Hi!" she said. She had her red hair in braids and her smile that always made me smile back. Buster was on his feet, straddling Sarah and wagging his tail in Newt's face, and Newt said, "Howdy, Louise. Buster, settle down," and he put the truck in gear and we were on our way.

"Thought we'd do a little target practice out in the cornfield and have a cookout in the back yard afterwards. Sound good by you two?"

"Uh-huh," Sarah said. She nudged me with her elbow, lifted her chin, and put on her angelic face, the way she did in church when she was up to something her mom wouldn't like.

"I never did target practice before. I never even fired a gun. But my dad has one in his work truck. He uses it only to shoot rabid foxes and skunks, though."

"Nothing to it," Newt said.

"My dad's coming home Monday," I told Newt. I wanted them to make friends so Newt would bring Sarah to Marl Lake. "Maybe you could meet him."

"I'd like that. Like to hear about his trip."

"Will your dad get to write another article?" Sarah asked.

"Oh, yeah, but for *National Geographic*? I think if he does a really good job he will."

"Then will you come back and stay with Aunt Kay and Uncle Jack again?"

I hesitated. If my dad took another trip, I was going with him. "My dad doesn't have to go away for me to come visit. Plus, we always come for Thanksgiving. But you can come to Marl Lake.

We'll take the canoe downstream and have a picnic on the bank. It's really cool. The stream flows from one lake to the next, and when you come around a bend, if you're really quiet, you might see something, like a bear or a deer with a fawn. One time I surprised an eagle, sitting on a branch right over the water. He was so close I could see his yellow eyes and when he pushed off the branch it cracked like a gunshot. His wings beat so hard they made ripples on the water and I could hear his feathers move against the air."

"I can't wait!" Sarah said. "Dad, can we go?"

"Sure we can. We'll bring our gear and camp out and do some fishing along the way. Make a nice trip out of it." Buster whapped Newt's leg with his tail and Newt patted his rump. "You love a road trip, don't you, boy?"

Newt's house was what my dad would call ranch style, maybe a mile or so off the highway. When we pulled into the driveway it looked to me like the garage was so big it made up half the house. Newt had turned it into a workshop for taxidermy.

"Here's where I work when I'm not at work," he said. Buster went over to a folded-up quilt in the corner and lay down. Next to Buster's bed there was a big wooden cabinet with glass doors. Inside it were all kinds of animals. There was a red fox, a weasel, a skunk, a pheasant, even a possum, all with glass eyes that stared.

"Most of those were roadkill from when I was learning my trade," Newt said. "Except for that one up there." He pointed to the head of a buck with antlers, hanging on the wall. "I got him on a trip up north. A clean shot through the heart. Kept the meat good and sweet, huh, Sarah?"

Sarah rolled her eyes. "Sure, Dad."

Newt laughed. "Sarah doesn't care for venison."

"I like venison chili," she said.

I could smell bleach and something like glue and I looked around the garage. Two big freezers stood against one wall and a workbench ran the length of another, with long fluorescent lights hanging over it. Spools of thread, curved needles, and funny-shaped knives lay spread out across the workbench, and on the wall behind it was a corkboard with notes and slips of paper pinned up and lots of pictures of Sarah.

Sarah hopped onto a stool. "Here's a picture of me when I just turned two," she said, pointing at a picture of a redheaded baby in a puffy white dress. "And that's from when we went camping out west and saw a grizzly bear."

I looked at the bear in the photograph. He was brown and shaggy, not like the black bears back home, and he was facing the camera.

"Weren't you scared?" I asked.

"Nah. They won't bother you as long as you stick to the park rules."

I shuddered because I'd heard stories about grizzly bears and people. I wondered how Sarah could be scared of a tiny little snake and not a huge bear that could eat you.

"Did you ever stuff a bear?" I asked Newt.

"No—anything bigger than a deer I don't handle. Most people want a bearskin rug anyway."

Sarah spun around on the stool, kicking out her feet. "Dad, I'm hungry."

"Well, let's fix up some lunch, then."

In the kitchen Newt put out packages of cold cuts and cheese, mustard, mayonnaise, bread, a jar of dill pickles, and some lettuce. He put everything on the table with plates and napkins and we made our own sandwiches the way we liked. I kept looking into the living room, where something had caught my eye. I realized that it was a large bird, perched on the mantel over the fireplace.

Newt saw me staring. "Go have a look at him, Louise."

I wiped my hands on my napkin and stood up from the table

and I went into the living room, almost tiptoeing, though I knew the bird wasn't alive. Perched on the mantel, looking down at me, he was bigger than Cash. It was hard to look away from his huge golden eyes, even though they were only glass. He had tufts of feathers like ears sticking up and furry-looking feathers on his feet that partly covered his talons. I was afraid to ask Newt if he had killed the owl.

Sarah came and stood beside me. "He almost seems alive."

"That poor fellow got tangled in a barbed-wire fence," Newt said. "He was swooping down on dinner. When I found him, it was too late."

"Why do people want stuffed animals?" I asked.

"Louise, good question. In my experience, people want trophies, mostly. It's a way to possess a little wilderness. Like folks who come back from the islands with trophy fish. They want to preserve the memory of battling that fish on the open sea."

Behind Newt's house was a cornfield that belonged to the farmer up the road. The cornfield stretched out like a square in a great quilt, with patches of woods on three sides. The woods were not the kind we had back home. I couldn't see any birch or pine trees, only maple and oak and ones like the raccoon tree. Newt said he had permission to look for arrowheads in the field, and also to hunt in the woods.

"What do you hunt?" I asked.

"Nothing, really. There's no game around here. But now and then I bag a rabbit and fix myself a nice stew."

I thought about the baby rabbit I'd held, back at Creekside Court. I knew that rabbits were food for a lot of animals. And I'd just eaten a sandwich with roast turkey on it. I didn't think I had a right to judge hunting and killing, but I hated it.

We walked into the field, each of us in our own path between rows of corn that came up past our waists. The long, broad leaves were such a bright green I had to squint, even in the hot, hazy air. Buster ran out ahead of us, leading the way. Sarah carried a sack of tin cans and Newt carried his gun.

I heard a high-pitched screech and saw a red-tailed hawk flying overhead, all white and brown speckled underneath. Three crows were diving and pecking at him from all sides, forcing him to fly in a jagged pattern, dipping down, then up, tilting to one side and another. The crows made growling caws and flew in wild angles, attacking the hawk again and again, while the big bird made his way across the sky.

A fourth crow followed, trying to catch up. Out the corner of my eye I saw Newt raise his gun, and there was a loud *crack!* The fourth crow stopped flapping his wings and he fell, tumbling, wings floppy, down into the cornstalks. Everything had gone silent. The other three crows and the hawk had disappeared, and no birds sang. There was only the buzz of cicadas coming from the trees. I started running to where the crow had fallen, and Buster ran too, faster than me. "No, Buster!" I yelled.

I heard Newt call the dog back and then I saw the still, black body up ahead and I kept running. I didn't know why I was in a hurry; it wasn't like he was going to fly away. I dropped to my knees. The crow was so much bigger on the ground than in the air. His wings were spread, his head was bent to the side, and his black eyes were wide open. I looked into them and for one second I thought, *Maybe he's alive, maybe he's just knocked out. Maybe if I just toss him up in the air, he'll fly.* I slid my hands under him. He felt warm and heavy. Holding his head in one hand, his body in the other, I lifted him onto my lap. His bill was open a little. I wished he would peck at me, the way the heron did. I folded one wing to his body, then the other, and I smoothed his feathers.

Newt squatted beside me. "He's big."

Sarah stood holding Buster's collar. "What should we do with him, Dad?"

"I want him," I said. "I'm going to take him home and bury him next to Cash." I didn't really believe their souls would meet up in heaven, or anything like that. But I wanted the crow. I felt a tear at the corner of my eye and I wiped it away quickly.

Sarah rubbed my shoulder. Buster wagged his tail and Newt said, "Be still, Buster. Now, Louise, don't cry."

"Were you going to eat him?" I asked.

"Course not," Newt said.

"Then why'd you kill him?"

"They were harassing the hawk."

"So?"

Newt ran a hand through his hair and looked at the ground. "I guess that's a lame excuse. Fact is, I did it without thinking much at all. I had a clean shot at him. When I was a boy on the farm, that's what we did. We shot crows."

"But why?"

"Louise, I can't explain."

I knew my dad could. When he came home he would explain it to me and then maybe I could understand.

Newt stood and put the gun strap over his shoulder. I got up with the crow in my arms, ignoring the hand Newt had put out to help me.

I walked in my own path between the cornstalks. When we got back to the house I said, "Can I please have something to wrap him in?"

Newt stood there a second. Then he said, "Louise, I am sorry. If I'd known it was going to upset you, I wouldn't have shot that crow."

We looked at each other and I thought his eyes really were sad. He took the gun strap off his shoulder and put the gun away.

"What would you say to letting me stuff him for you? I could make him look like he was flying, or like he just landed on a branch."

"I don't know. Maybe."

Sarah and I looked at each other. She raised her eyebrows as if to say, *Why not?*

Newt went in the house and came back with a white towel.

"Thanks," I said. I spread the towel on the ground. Buster came to see.

"Lie down, boy," Newt said.

I leaned forward and let the crow come away from my chest, cradling his head. I laid him on the towel and folded one side and then the other to cover him completely. Then I took the bundle in my arms and stood up. "Could you take me home now?"

"Sure," Newt said. "Sarah, grab us some Cokes out of the fridge."

CROW SMELL

At first we were quiet on the ride back. I held on to my crow and watched cars go by out the window. I could smell him. He had a special smell, an animal smell, clean. Like stone and sky and feathers, but not like other birds' feathers, not like a robin or the heron. Like a *crow*.

Newt had said that he shot crows when he was a boy, but he was a grownup now. I couldn't put it together with how he was at the zoo, with the butterflies. But I knew that I shouldn't be mad at Newt. Besides, if he hadn't shot the crow, I wouldn't be holding him. Right then I hated myself for loving the way his warm, feathered body felt against me and for the way I always wished I could hold a wild crow.

"Back home," I said, "I have a garden."

"You do?" Newt said.

"Uh-huh. And my dad and I make compost. But a lot of the stuff we put on the pile doesn't go into the compost, because our crows get it."

"'Our' crows?" Sarah said.

"Yes. They live in our woods and build their nests and raise their families there. They watch and they know when I bring out the bucket with scraps. One of them, a scout, caws three times to call in the whole family, and after I dump the bucket I go inside the cottage to watch. The scout flies in for a closer look, and if there's really good stuff, like fish heads or a mouse that Cash caught, he calls again, loud, and crows swoop down from the trees and take the food."

"They're more complicated than I thought," Newt said. "So you made a study of them?"

"I just watch them. I'm pretty sure I know what they're doing, most of the time. Like when they play. I've seen two crows play tug-of-war with a twig. And one time I heard a funny clicking sound, like winding up an old clock. I looked up and saw a crow hanging upside down under a branch, swinging and clicking. I know he was playing."

"You didn't tell me about the crows before," Sarah said.

It was true; I hadn't talked about my crows back home. I didn't know why.

For the whole ride, Buster kept still, with his head down in Newt's lap. Sarah put her head on my shoulder and I rested my head against hers. My arms grew numb from holding the crow so tight. I loosened my grip and they tingled, trying to wake up. Newt put on the turn signal and we exited the highway.

Sarah asked, "What will you tell Aunt Kay?"

"Nothing. I don't want her to see him."

When Newt parked in front of the house I said I was sorry for asking to come home before the cookout.

"No matter," Newt said. "Plenty of cookouts ahead. Will you think about letting me stuff that crow for you?"

"I will," I said, not sure. I needed to talk to my dad about it all. I got out of the truck with the bundled crow under my arm and said goodbye to Sarah.

I went up the steps into the house and was halfway up the stairs when Aunt Kay said, "Hello, dear. You're home early. Is everything all right?"

"Oh, yes, Aunt Kay."

"That laundry? I'll take it and put it right in. I'm just starting a load now."

"No, it's just my swimsuit in here, and nothing's dirty. I'll hang it in the shower."

"All right, then. Come tell me about your day. I just took a chocolate cake out of the oven."

"I'll be right down." I hurried the rest of the way up the stairs and into my room and I shut the door. I set the bundle on the bed and unwrapped my crow and ran my hands over his limp, feathered body, under his wings and around his back and neck and head. When I couldn't find a bullet hole I thought, *Then he can't really be dead.* But I knew better.

Downstairs, the phone rang. I felt like I should go visit with my Aunt Kay. There were sudden footsteps right outside my door and I scrunched up the blankets to hide my crow, just as Aunt Kay knocked and came in. "Louise," she said. Her face was pale and worried. "A call from the *Geographic* office. It's Jeff. The infection is worse."

"I want to talk to him."

"We can't. He's in intensive care now."

"When is he coming home?"

Aunt Kay came to put her arms around me.

"When is my dad coming home?" I asked again.

"We don't know. Why not come downstairs with me and I'll fix us both some cocoa."

"I don't want any."

Aunt Kay held my face in her hands and kissed my forehead. Her eyes were moist. "Your father is strong," she said. "He will be all right."

"I feel sick. Can I go to bed?"

"Of course, dear. Climb under the covers and I'll check on you later and see if you're hungry." She went out and pulled the door shut behind her.

I sat down on the bed and uncovered my crow and stared into his eyes while mine kept filling up and spilling over. "Dad's not coming home," I told him.

After a while I put my head down on the pillow and pulled my crow close and covered us with a blanket. I held on to him and stroked his soft wings. My tears wetted his feathers and his crow smell got stronger.

When I woke up it was light in the room and my nose was all stuffed. I remembered about my dad and then I came awake fast and my heart sped up when I felt my bare feet. I didn't remember taking off my sneakers. I reached for my crow and I saw that the blanket still covered him. Surely Aunt Kay hadn't seen.

I pushed back the blanket and sat up in bed and wiped my face. There was a little dried blood on my hands. I lifted my crow onto my lap. He felt cold and his eyes had turned dull and I wondered if I ought to shut them. Before, I hadn't wanted to stop looking into them, as if he could see me somehow. He was stiff and his claws curled as if grasping for a branch. I gave him my finger to hold on to and petted his wings with my other hand. Yesterday I had been able to unfold one and see the soft, smoky gray feathers underneath. Now his wings were fixed against his body and his head stayed to one side, as if he were looking over his shoulder.

My Aunt Kay tapped on the door. "May I come in?"

I pushed my crow back under the covers and said yes.

"It's Sarah calling," she said, bringing me the phone. She looked so worried and I felt sorry, even though I hadn't really done anything wrong.

"Thanks, Aunt Kay," I said.

"You look feverish."

"I'm okay. I'll come downstairs in a minute."

Aunt Kay left and I put the phone to my ear. "Hello?"

"It's Sarah. Are you coming to church with us?"

"My dad has an infection and he's not coming home."

"Oh, no, Louise! He's going to be okay, though, right?"

I couldn't answer.

"Well, he will," Sarah said firmly.

I couldn't help but smile. I gripped the phone and wiped my nose on my wrist.

"Louise," Sarah said. "Come to church with us."

After a moment I said, "I'll be ready when you get here."

I pulled my bag down from the closet shelf, wrapped my crow in Dad's old U of M sweatshirt, tucked him inside the bag, and zipped it shut. I put on my dress and sandals and my tortoise necklace, and I checked Cash's collar on my wrist to make sure it was buckled.

"You've packed a bag," Aunt Kay said.

"It's just a sweatshirt in case I get cold."

"Dear, it's ninety degrees out."

"Sometimes they have the air conditioner turned way up."

Aunt Kay put her hand on my forehead and my cheek. "You feel warm. Are you coming down with something? Maybe we better take you to the doctor."

"I'm okay."

"Poor dear, I know you're worried about your father. I am too. Come have breakfast."

"I'm not really hungry. Anyway, Sarah will be here soon."

I sat in the chair by the window to wait. Aunt Kay brought me a glass of orange juice. "I don't want you getting sick."

"Don't worry, Aunt Kay." I drank the juice down and gave her the empty glass.

The white Buick pulled up in front of the house and I climbed in beside Sarah. She said, "What's in—" and stopped herself, because she knew.

"It's a sweatshirt in case I get cold."

Mrs. Hickerson said, "It's ninety degrees outside."

"I know. In case the air conditioning's too high."

"Sarah tells me your father is ill. I'm very sorry to hear it. We will pray for him."

"Thank you, Mrs. Hickerson." I looked at Sarah out the corner of my eye. She nudged me with her knee.

"You girls always have your secrets, don't you?"

"Mom, I'm trying to cheer Louise up. Stop being suspicious."

We sat in the same place, halfway from the front, left side of the aisle, middle of the pew, first me, then Sarah, then her mother. The minister stood at the podium, opened his Bible, and began to speak. Soon his voice faded. I tried to imagine the hospital bed my dad was in and the people who were taking care of him. Were they being extra nice and trying to make him well? I wondered where my mother was and why she stayed away. I knew she hadn't been ready for a family when I happened. Dad had explained it to me. "We were living in the city when your mother became pregnant with you," he said, "and she had a job she loved more than anything." Dad never said a thing about her that wasn't nice, and he never acted mad. But I was mad, because now he was sick and where was she? How could she know if we were okay when she never wrote or called?

I wanted to be home in our cottage. I wanted to hear my dad's voice saying things would turn out all right, like the time he got the flu and couldn't get out of bed for two days. I brought him cups of ginger tea with honey and covered him with blankets. I built up the fire in the stove and then I turned on the oven and went to work making bread. The whole cottage filled with the smell, and when it was done, I brought my dad a hot slice with butter. He couldn't eat it, but he breathed in the steamy, buttery slice and he said, "Everything's going to be all right, Lews."

Sarah put her hand over mine and squeezed. A heavy feeling came into my throat and I couldn't swallow and the corners of my eyes stung. Sarah kept a hold on my hand and I didn't want her to let go, even though it was going to make me cry. I looked up at the ceiling and shut my eyes, but they kept stinging and then a hot tear slipped out and rolled down my face. I snuck my free hand up to wipe it away before anyone could see. Mrs. Hickerson pulled out a Kleenex from her purse and passed it to me. The minister stopped talking and all the people bowed heads and I did too.

They Stay All Year Round

Aunt Kay was in my room when I got home from church. "Louise, when I changed the sheets on your bed I found this." She held up a black feather.

It was useless to lie. "Newt shot a crow Saturday."

"What? Are you telling me you had a dead crow in the house? In your bed?"

My heart thumped in my chest.

"Is it in that bag? Louise, you cannot carry around a dead bird." Aunt Kay shook her head. "My goodness, and you were feverish just this morning. Haven't we got our hands full, with Jeff in the hospital so far away? I can't be worrying about you catching some disease from a dead bird, if you haven't already!"

It was the first time I'd heard my Aunt Kay raise her voice. I stood holding the bag with my crow inside pressed against me.

"What did you think you were going to do with a dead crow?" she demanded.

"Have him, Aunt Kay! Just have him. I'm alone here! Maybe if you weren't allergic to everything alive, Cash wouldn't be dead. What if Dad never comes home? I can't live here forever!" I turned and ran down the stairs and out the door.

I ran out the driveway, through the main gate, and up the sidewalk to my special place. At the end of the sidewalk I quit running and walked down the path, my heart thudding in my chest. I sat down under the raccoon tree, unzipped the bag, and took out my crow. His wings were limp and his head hung loose. The rigor mortis had broken and he was starting to stink. I couldn't hold on to him anymore and smell his crow smell; all I could do was look at him, at his inky black feathers and claws curled up and eyes sunken in.

I tried to gather his wings to his body, but they kept falling open. His body felt lighter, though. It had to be drying out, which was good, because then he'd stop stinking. Maybe I could hide him in the raccoon tree until he dried out. Maybe he would dry out like the woodpecker that hit the window one time.

I remembered the crack of the woodpecker's head hitting the glass. He had screeched and cried and shook in my hands, and his head was bent to the side. I knew his neck was broken and he was hurting and I yelled, "No, don't die! Stop!" and then he just quit screeching and lay still with his head hanging loose and his eyes half shut. His eyelids were gray naked skin. I held him in my hands, my whole body hunched over him, my face in his feathers, and I couldn't stop sobbing, it just hurt so much. Finally I did stop, and I started to touch his black-and-white-patterned wings and the red spot on the back of his head and his long bill that was like dark, polished wood. I kept the woodpecker in my room on the windowsill, with the window open. In the sun and the breeze he gradually dried out. His eyes became hollow and his body was light and didn't stink anymore.

I leaned against the raccoon tree and listened to a robin singing the way they do in the late afternoon, when the air is still and hot and their babies are gone from the nest. I felt so tired and I shut my eyes.

When I woke up, ants were clustered around my crow's eyes. I started smacking them away and then realized I was being cruel to creatures who were only doing their job, so I stopped. I heard voices and fast, light footsteps, and suddenly Buster was there, licking my face.

"I knew you'd be here," Sarah said. "Your Aunt Kay and Uncle Jack are really worried about you, but I told them I knew where you'd be."

A shiver went through my stomach because I was in trouble for running away. "What're you doing here?" I asked Newt.

"Sarah told me you brought that crow to church," Newt said. "Your Aunt Kay is pretty upset about you toting around a big dead bird. I'm responsible for that. And we're going to have to bury him, or stuff him."

I couldn't think of where to bury him. Not in Aunt Kay and Uncle Jack's yard. And not where we were, in my special place, because when they made a new development in the field, they'd cut down the raccoon tree and dig up everything, like with Creekside Court. "If it's not too late," I said, "can we stuff him?"

"Sure can," Newt said. He squatted beside me and held out his hands. We looked at each other and I gave him my crow. Gently, Newt folded the bird's wings to his body, wrapped him in the sweatshirt, and put him in the bag. "Let's go on home and let your family know you're all right."

We started walking back to the house. Sarah said, "Aunt Kay thinks you hate it here, with her and Uncle Jack."

"She doesn't understand. How long will it take to stuff him?" I asked Newt.

"Not long. I'll bring him when I come down to pick up Sarah in two weeks to do her school shopping."

I thought about how I was supposed to be home by then, getting ready to start at my own school.

Aunt Kay and Uncle Jack were waiting on the steps, and when Aunt Kay saw us she rushed to meet us. "Oh heavens, oh dear! There you are." She put her arms around me and held on tight. When she pulled back I saw how red her eyes were.

"I'm sorry, Aunt Kay."

She kept an arm around me and we walked slowly to Uncle Jack, standing at the steps with his hands on his waist.

"Sorry, Uncle Jack," I said.

"We'd better get going," Newt said.

Uncle Jack shook Newt's hand. "Thank you for coming."

Newt put the bag with my crow in the back of his truck and then he opened the passenger side door. Buster jumped in first and Sarah followed. Newt got in and started the truck. Sarah leaned out the window. "Call me later."

Newt put the truck in gear and they drove away.

"Poor dear," Aunt Kay said. "You must be starving."

"I was only gone a few hours."

"Go in the kitchen," Uncle Jack said. "Let your aunt feed you."

I sat at the table while my Aunt Kay warmed a plate of food in the microwave. When it beeped, she took out the steaming plate and set it down in front of me and I remembered that I hadn't eaten all day. I said thank you and picked up my fork and dug into the chicken potpie she'd made from scratch.

Aunt Kay fussed at the sink and wiped the countertops and then she poured herself an iced tea and sat down at the table with me. She cleared her throat. "I have been thinking—"

"Aunt Kay," I interrupted. "I don't hate it here. But I miss Dad and Marl Lake and my cat. It's not your fault he got killed. I'm sorry for saying that."

"I know, dear. And I'm sorry I was so unkind about your crow. Please understand that I have to think of your well-being."

"Crows have been near since I was little, since I can remember. There's a whole family and they live right there in our woods in Marl Lake, and they come when I bring out food and I'm happy when I hear them calling."

Aunt Kay listened to me the way she always did, a hundred percent.

"They stay all year round, year after year, and they never go away." My eyes stung. "What if he dies, Aunt Kay?" I picked up my dinner napkin to wipe my face, and Aunt Kay patted my hand. She scooted her chair close and put her arms around me.

"Your father is going to be fine, I feel sure of it," she said. "These kinds of illnesses take time."

After a moment she pulled back so we could see each other. She brushed the wet off my cheek with her thumb. "I was thinking that we might find you a pet."

"But how would that work? What about your allergies?"

Aunt Kay raised her eyebrows. "I'm not allergic to turtles."

THREE-LEGGED TORTOISE

Aunt Kay took me to a pet shop the very next day. There were painted turtles, the same kind that were in Marl Lake. The turtles sat on a fake branch, basking under a fluorescent light. A filter bubbled in the water. Inside another tank were six little tortoises almost as round as golf balls.

"Those are baby red foots," the salesman said. "Very nice pets. Easy to care for."

"My goodness," Aunt Kay said, peering over the top of her glasses. "They really are cute. What do you think, Louise? You should have two so they keep each other company."

"They're adorable," I said. Two of them could sit in the palm of my hand. It would be so much fun to care for the tiny babies and to watch them grow up. "What kind of turtle is that?" I asked, pointing to a tank on the bottom shelf.

"You don't want him," the salesman said. "He's missing a leg."

"Really?" I knelt in front of the tank to get a closer look at the plain brown-shelled tortoise, who had pressed himself into the corner and was maybe asleep. He was the size and shape of a box turtle. Newspaper was spread on the bottom of the tank. A red plastic water bowl and scraps of apple were scattered around.

"Which leg is missing?" I asked. "What happened?"

"The back leg on the left. We don't know, but what I think is, he had a run-in with a dog. There are scratches in the shell that look an awful lot like tooth marks."

I shuddered to think of how that must have hurt, to have a dog bite off his leg. "Can I hold him?"

"Well, okay," the salesman said. He took off the screened lid.

"Can I?"

"Go ahead."

I slid my hand under the tortoise and lifted him out. He felt heavy and that was good. The wild turtles I held were always heavy, and that meant they were healthy. I turned the tortoise around so I could see him. He kept his head in his shell, but his round, brown eyes were open and they were looking right back at me. He was afraid, but curious, too. "I want him."

"Are you sure you wouldn't rather have baby red foots?" the salesman asked.

"I'm sure. Hello, tortoise," I whispered. "Don't be scared." I looked at his scaly legs that were tucked back under his shell, like armored pillars. I touched the nub of skin-covered bone where his back leg was supposed to be. The skin felt dry and smooth, like a callus on my dad's hand.

"Well, then," Aunt Kay said, "we'll take the three-legged tortoise. And please, if you would, help us with whatever he needs. One of those large aquariums, I think. And the lights and a water bowl. And we'll need some sort of care guide. You have one, don't you?"

"Yes," the salesman said, and went about collecting the things.

"You're sure he's what you want, dear?"

"I'm sure."

I held the tortoise close. For the ride home, he sat in my lap, because I didn't want him to be put in a box. I wanted him to feel safe and like nothing bad would ever happen to him again.

Uncle Jack carried the big tank up the stairs and into my room. He put the tank on the desk and brushed off his hands.

"Thanks, Uncle Jack," I said.

He patted my shoulder. "I'm glad you and your Aunt Kay worked things out."

I found a picture of my tortoise in the care guide. Under the photo it said, *Russian tortoise: A hardy species that tolerates cold weather.*

I didn't want my tortoise to have to tolerate anything. "It's cold at Marl Lake during winter," I told him. "We'll go back one day. But I'll keep you warm, I promise."

The care guide also said that tortoises liked to eat grass. Uncle Jack didn't spray the grass in the back yard; he just cut it a lot. So at dinner I asked him, "Can we let a patch of grass grow for my tortoise?"

"You bet we can. Just show me where."

I pointed to a spot in the corner of the yard near the roses. There was enough new growth to make a little shade, if my tortoise got too hot.

It was the hardest thing not to hold my tortoise, just to let him be, so he could get used to his new home. I brought him chopped-up collard greens and dandelions and watermelon. He even ate the watermelon rind. When he was done he reached forward with his front foot and squeezed his eyes shut and wiped his face until the sticky juice was off.

Finally after a few days I took my tortoise outside one morning, so he could walk around in the sunshine and nibble on the patch of grass Uncle Jack let grow. I rested my hand on his shell. It felt like wood that was worn smooth by many hands. Soon his nose poked out. Then his head came out all the way, stretching his neck to see around the yard. He blinked and looked at the ground. Then he lowered his head and began to eat the grass, biting and tugging, tearing with the stubby claws on his front legs. Everything he did, he did slowly, as if being careful. But he could pull himself into his shell fast if something scared him, like my Uncle Jack walking across the yard.

"Got your new friend, have you?" He stood with his hands in his pockets and his sun visor on.

"Uh-huh. He's kind of shy."

"We must look like giants to him. How do we know that he is a he?"

"His shell underneath. The book says it's called a plastron, and in males it's a little bit cupped. The female's plastron is flat. I guess that's so eggs will fit better inside."

"I see."

My tortoise had gotten over being scared of Uncle Jack and was walking toward the fence. His shell tipped forward and then back with each step, and his short tail hung down thin and pointy. I had the urge to rush over and gather him up and hold on to him. But I didn't want to spoil his fun.

"Wounded in battle, was he?"

"By a dog. That's what the pet store man said."

"I wonder if he can get under that fence and out of the yard."

"Yeah, I'm going to have to watch him all the time when he's outside." I stood up to go catch him, because even though he only had three legs, he was moving kind of fast.

"Looks like he needs some sort of pen."

"How could we make one?"

"Well, can he climb?"

"Not like up a tree or anything."

"Then all we need is some boards."

I picked up my tortoise and followed Uncle Jack to the garage. He took off his sun visor and set it on the workbench. The garage was cool and the fluorescent lights made everything pale and a little blue. I held my tortoise in the palm of one hand and covered him with the other to keep him warm. From the stack of lumber scraps against the wall, Uncle Jack took four wide boards. He measured each one and then cut a little bit off the ends of two of them. Then he set the boards on the floor, up on their edges, so they made the frame of a pen.

"Now all we need to do is put hardware on the corners."

I set my tortoise down on an old packing blanket inside a box so I could help. I held the boards in place while Uncle Jack fitted the brackets on the corners and screwed them in. He stood and looked at the four boards bracketed together. "Will he dig his way out?"

"He might."

Uncle Jack pulled out four more boards and cut them and screwed them onto the frame to make a sort of ledge that went around the inside. "That should keep him from digging his way out."

The sun was directly overhead when we carried the pen outside. We set it on the grass near the roses so that the leafy new growth shaded one side. I ran back to the garage and got my tortoise and put him in the pen. Now he could walk around in there and eat the grass and sun himself, or he could go in the shade.

Aunt Kay brought us lemonade. "I'm glad you found something good to do with those old boards."

Uncle Jack said, "I think it's big enough for two turtles."

"He needs a friend of his own kind," I said.

"You got it, kiddo." He drank the rest of his lemonade, gave the glass to Aunt Kay, and kissed her on the cheek. "Gonna get my clippers and gloves and work on my roses." He patted my shoulder and went off to the garage.

Aunt Kay said, "We can ask at the pet shop about another tortoise."

"How does Uncle Jack know about tortoises?"

"I don't think he knows a ding-dong thing about tortoises, dear. But he knows about being loved and having someone to love."

On Saturday Newt came early, before picking up Sarah to go shopping. He brought my crow. He was perched on a branch, with his wings slightly raised as if landing or about to fly.

"He looks as though he might fly off any minute!" Aunt Kay said.

"Thank you," Newt said. "I am pleased with the way he turned out."

I ran my hand down the crow's back and across his tail feathers. I looked at his dark glass eyes and black bill. I put my face close to find his crow smell, but it was gone. Now he smelled like leather and a little like Newt's garage.

"Are you disappointed?" Newt asked.

"No, he's wonderful. It's just that I don't think I need him the way I thought I did."

"Well, I sure like him," Newt said.

"I want you to have him."

"I know where he goes, too, right on the mantel, scolding me not to shoot any more crows."

Marl Lake

The salesman at the pet shop said he would check with the herpeto-logical society adoptions committee to see if there were any Russian tortoises available. "If I am unable to locate one, would you like me to order one from a breeder?"

"Oh," Aunt Kay said. "Why, yes. Please. Do you mean to tell me that someone breeds these tortoises?"

"Indeed. Russian tortoises, red foots. Argentine horned frogs. Boa constrictors."

"My goodness! And these animals are for pets?"

"Yes, ma'am."

"How fascinating," she said, taking out her credit card.

The salesman wrote down the card information for a deposit. "And we're looking for a female?"

"Yes, please," I said.

The salesman gave the card back to Aunt Kay and she put it in her purse. "Well, there must be a lot more people with allergies to furry animals than I had imagined."

"Or people who like all kinds of pets," I said.

We left the pet shop and headed back toward the highway. Aunt Kay said, "Dear, we need to think about school."

"I know."

She patted my knee. "Since we're by the mall we ought to do a little shopping."

Late that afternoon I struggled through the front door with three big shopping bags of jeans, sweaters, shoes, and socks. Aunt Kay went back out to the car to get the new cake mixer she'd found on sale. I had started up the stairs with the bags when the phone rang. I left the bags on the stairs and ran back down to the kitchen to answer it.

"Hello. Miller residence."

"Lews?"

"Dad?"

"Yes, sweetheart, it's me."

"You're alive!"

He laughed. "Yes, I'm alive. Were you worried I might not be?"

"Well, yeah, kind of! Are you coming home?"

"In two days. I'll have to rest a night at home and then I'll drive down to get you."

Aunt Kay came in with her shopping bags and I yelled, "He's alive!" and started jumping up and down.

"Thank heavens!" she said, dropping the bags and clapping her hands together.

I could hear my dad laughing. "It's so good to hear your voice," he said. "You sound just fine. How are Kay and Jack?"

"They're great! Dad, I have so much to tell you. I have a tortoise! And a friend. Her name's Sarah. And I had a stuffed crow, but I gave him back."

"Well, I want to hear everything just as soon as I'm home. Right now I better get off the phone, though. I'll see you in just a few days, Lews. I can hardly wait. I love you."

"I love you too, Dad." I put down the phone and Aunt Kay and I hugged each other.

"Did he say when he could come home?"

"Two days! Then he said he has to rest overnight before driving down."

"I have a better idea. Perhaps Uncle Jack and I would enjoy a trip. It's been a long time since we went anyplace together. And I don't think it's good for Jeff to make that drive so soon after his illness."

"When can we leave?"

"Oh, I'll talk with Jack about it, but in a couple of days, I expect."

"What about my new tortoise?"

"I'll call the pet shop and arrange to have her sent directly to you."

Then I remembered that I was supposed to go with Sarah and Newt next Saturday, to the county fair. "I better call Sarah."

Mrs. Hickerson brought Sarah to spend the afternoon with me.

"Have you picked out a name?" Sarah asked. She knelt in the grass next to the pen, watching my tortoise eat the blackberries Aunt Kay bought at the market especially for him.

"Ivan," I said.

"Like Ivan the Terrible?"

"No, Ivan the Brave. He has to be brave to live with only three legs."

"Does he know you?"

"Maybe not the way Cash did. But we just met and he's already quit pulling into his shell when I touch him. The book says he could live a long time, and I'm going to take extra-good care of him. And guess what? We're getting a female tortoise."

"Will they have babies?"

"I don't know. Maybe."

"You gotta write me when they do. And send pictures."

"I will. You want to walk to the field? I think there might be wild blackberries to pick."

Sarah and I walked out of Creekside Court and up the sidewalk. Sarah said, "You never told me about your mother."

"She left when I was born."

"You don't see her? You don't know where she is?"

"No. She didn't want a family."

"Wow, that's too bad."

"It's okay. My dad takes good care of us. That's why he went to Brazil."

After I said it, I knew it was true. Maybe he wanted to see the rain forest and take an exciting trip, but I knew it was hard work too.

"He really wants to write a novel," I told Sarah. "But he said that wouldn't earn us a living. And I said, 'So? I can grow a garden and you can fish and hunt.' Then he said, 'What about money for college?' 'I'm not going to college,' I said. Whenever I say that he says, 'Oh yes you are.'"

"Maybe you and I can go to the same college."

"Hey, yeah, that would be cool!"

We came to the field that had been an empty lot. From the trees came a surge of cicada buzzing, loud, then quiet, then loud again in the thick, humid air. Sun-yellow sprays of goldenrod and round white discs of Queen Anne's lace bloomed across the field. Pale green pods fat with seeds had replaced the purple milkweed flowers. There were a lot more bumblebees than before, and they clustered around the flowers like they were in a hurry to get all the nectar they could. The weeds and wildflowers were so tall it was hard to see if there were any flat things to turn over. I let my fingers brush against some goldenrod and smelled the powdery yellow pollen. It smelled like honey and earth.

I tried to imagine how this place would be without Creekside Court and all the developments. I imagined thick woods of maple and oak and the trees Aunt Kay said were beech, though I liked to call them raccoon trees. There would be fields like the one we were in, filled with wildflowers and bees and crab spiders, and there would be ponds, I bet, full of frogs and tadpoles and herons, too. And if there were more trees, then crows might come and stay.

Back home, too, there was goldenrod blooming. But the air would be clear and dry and the sky extra blue, with high, puffy canoe-shaped clouds. The nights were getting cool and so was the lake water. And the crows born in the spring would be almost grown up. I knew the crows didn't go hungry all summer just because they didn't get our table scraps—they would fly all around Marl Lake and over the woods to find food. But what if they went far away and didn't come back?

Sarah and I walked to the briars by the trees and found some blackberries. We picked a handful each and sat down on the rocks under the raccoon tree.

"Dad wanted me to say goodbye," Sarah said. "And that you could count on us coming up for a visit and some fishing. He said he named your crow Mr. Krum."

"Who?"

"Mr. Krum, his fourth-grade teacher, who was always scolding him."

"Was your dad in trouble a lot?"

"He must've been."

I ate the last of my berries and crunched the tiny seeds. "Do you really, truly believe animals don't have souls?"

Sarah looked at the ground. "I don't know. Don't tell *anyone* I said that."

"I won't."

She leaned forward and drew a circle in the dirt with her finger. "I was thinking about it a lot. I believe the Bible, I do," she said. "But those butterflies at the zoo? And that cute little snake I held, and even the crow. I thought about what you told us about crows and their families. Then there's Ivan with his three legs. And Buster! How can he not have a soul? How could God make such creatures and keep them out of heaven and not give them souls?"

I smiled at Sarah. "I can't wait for you to come visit."

"Me too."

The cottage was quiet, the lake still, with no wind on the water, only ripples made by fish getting breakfast below the glassy surface, and bugs scooting along above. The sky was pale pink where the sun was coming up. A phoebe swooped down from a pine bough to get a fly. The phoebes hadn't started to migrate yet. But they were quiet; they didn't say, *Phoebe!* Their babies had all grown up.

I heard someone in the kitchen below, putting on the kettle. I climbed out of bed, pulled on jeans and a T-shirt, and crept down the stairs. Uncle Jack was still asleep on the couch that opens into a bed. Dad had tried to make them take his room, but they refused.

I saw Aunt Kay by the stove in her pink bathrobe and matching slippers. "Good morning, sunshine," she whispered. "I'm going to miss you." Her eyes teared up and mine did too. We hugged each other. They were leaving after lunch and driving halfway, to the Holiday Inn. Then they would drive the rest of the way home in the morning.

"I'll come visit," I said.

"I'm counting on it. Now, what shall we make for breakfast?"

"Everything."

"Everything it is."

We made pancakes and bacon and eggs and fried potatoes. Dad came out of his bedroom. "Wow," he said, sniffing the air. "Bacon."

I knew it would be a long time before we had bacon again—probably the next time I saw Aunt Kay and Uncle Jack. Dad was skinnier than normal, but I didn't worry, because he had eaten seconds of everything Aunt Kay had cooked since we got home three days earlier. She had cleaned the whole cottage, and I helped stack firewood that Dad and Uncle Jack split.

At dinner the night before, Uncle Jack had made a toast to Dad's article. "And here's to the next one," he said.

Aunt Kay said, "I wonder where they will send you."

"*If* they send me," Dad said. "But I think there will be more work. Thankfully, by the time I got sick, we'd finally seen jaguars. I had enough to finish my piece."

Dad and I exchanged glances. He had promised that there would be stories to tell, and I could hardly wait. The next time he went to the rain forest to write an article I hoped I could go too. Aunt Kay and Uncle Jack said they would babysit my tortoises. But if Dad really needed to go on his own, that would be okay.

Dad and Uncle Jack built another pen in my room, for Ivan and my new tortoise, who would come any day. I decided to name her Brazil. Ivan liked our sandy, scruffy yard even though it didn't have much grass he could eat. What he really liked was the garden. I took him inside the fence and set him down. He was getting so used to me picking him up that he didn't pull into his shell anymore. I always told him where we were going, just so he could hear my voice. As soon as I set him down in the garden he nodded his head up and down the way he did when he was excited. Off he went on his three legs, his shell tilting and rocking. He stopped to eat the leaves on the bean plants and then he took a bite out of a yellow squash that had gotten too big to pick. He ate some of the kale that was all bolted and wild-looking, and next, he nibbled on the carrot tops. In the spring Dad and I would check the fence and fix any places where tortoises could get out.

After lunch Dad and I stood in the driveway waving goodbye to Aunt Kay and Uncle Jack. Soon their car was out of sight behind the pine trees and I couldn't hear the tires on the gravel anymore. I almost felt sad, and that was funny, because I was finally home where I had wanted to be.

"I want to visit Cash," I said. I felt my wrist where Cash's collar had been all summer. I'd put it on my bookshelf.

We went to where he was buried, between the garden and the edge of the woods. Mr. Lee had marked it with a ring of smooth stones from Marl Lake.

"We can plant a tree here if you want to," Dad said.

"Yes. One that stays green all year round. One the crows will nest in someday."

I didn't have a mouse for the crows. But there were chicken bones and mashed potatoes and corn, and there was one piece left of the chocolate cake that Aunt Kay had made. I put it all in the bucket and took it out to the compost heap. Wilted weeds that the Lees had pulled from the garden covered old compost and on top of that were eggshells, bread crusts, tea leaves, melon rinds, and stuff from our first few days home. Setting aside the chocolate cake, I lifted the bucket and dumped it, letting the handle bang against it. I called out, *Cah! Cah! Cah!* and my heart filled up and I stood very still and listened into the distance, into the woods and all around as far as I could. Then suddenly I heard, *Cah! Cah! Cah!* right across Marl Lake. An answer came from the trees not far away; then another crow called out. I felt as though they had been there all along, waiting.

CPSIA information can be obtained at www.ICGtesting.com
261564BV00002B/1/P